# CHAPTER 1

*S*even-year-old Elizabeth Green experienced trauma early in life. She grew up living in the apartment above her family's button shop in Birmingham with her mother and father, and although their family kept to themselves and she had no other relatives to speak of, she never felt lonely and always knew she was loved as long as her parents were beside her. Her mother Lily was a gentlehearted woman with a smile for everyone. She regarded even the rudest of customers at the button shop with empathy, imagining the difficulties they must have been enduring to upset them so much, and telling Elizabeth that she should always look for the best in people, and forgive them their mistakes.

Her father Samuel was generally a quiet, hardworking man, but he offered his family a steady sort of love and care that never left any room to doubt his devotion to them.

Elizabeth took after both her parents in her own way. She was a quiet child, too, preferring to hum songs to herself over going outside to find others to play with, but she was curious too, and she listened to every word spoken in her presence with a careful consideration that suggested she never planned to forget a single thing she had heard. Life in a button shop was not what most people would consider glamorous, but the buttons were like jewels to Elizabeth's eyes, a sparkling, multi-coloured treasure that she got to play with every day. She loved seeing fancy people's clothes, when they brought in their gowns and jackets for their buttons to be replaced, and she loved sitting beside her mother as she taught her how to mend a tear so that you couldn't see a single stitch, or to reattach a button so that it would never fall off again.

"But don't we want it to fall off?" Elizabeth had asked her. "Otherwise they won't come back."

"We want to be as good as we can to our customers," her mother said patiently. "It would be wrong to do a poor job to force them to spend more money. And besides, if our buttons always fall off, they'll go elsewhere. If our buttons are steady and trustworthy, like we aim to be, they'll always come back when they need something new."

Elizabeth also loved seeing her father at work, so focussed and peaceful looking, with a glint in his eye that told the world how much pride he took in his craft. She was not allowed to help make any of the buttons, for her father was a perfectionist in his work and he thought Elizabeth far too young, but she loved to watch her father and see the proud little smile that would gently spread across his face when he finished a job well done.

But one day, Elizabeth's mother went out in the early evening to deliver some completed work to a customer and did not return. Elizabeth waited up for her in the front of the shop while her father worked on a few more orders, watching the lamplighter pass by with his work and the streets gradually darken as night fell. When her father finally looked up from his work, it was fully dark, and her mother was beyond late. It must have been past dinner time, because Elizabeth's stomach growled with hunger, but she continued to sit by the shop

# THE LOST ORPHANS OF DARK STREETS

RACHEL DOWNING

# THE BUTTON MAKER'S ORPHAN DAUGHTER

## THE LOST ORPHANS OF DARK STREETS: PART I

window, looking at the now-empty street for any sign of her mother.

"Still not back yet?" her father said as he walked up to stand beside her. He kept his tone mild, but Elizabeth thought she heard a little worry in there, too. She shook her head, and her father sighed. "Maybe she got waylaid," he said. "Mrs. Higgins is the sort of customer who likes to talk. Your mother probably knows about the history and condition of every one of her dogs by now. She'll be home soon."

But her father did not sound convinced. They locked up the shop and headed upstairs, knowing that her mother had a key, but her father refused to eat supper until she was home, leaving Elizabeth to sit by the window, stomach rumbling, watching for any sign of her mother's return.

She nodded off, waiting, and woke up around midnight to her father's gentle hand on her shoulder. "Elizabeth," he murmured. "I'm going out. I'll be back soon."

"Where are you going?" Elizabeth murmured. "Where's mama?"

"She'll be home soon," her father said. "You wait here for her, all right?"

Elizabeth nodded, rubbing the sleep from her eyes, and her father squeezed her shoulder one more time before leaving. Her stomach felt completely empty now, so she took a candle to the kitchen and grabbed a small piece of bread. After thinking for a moment, she walked back downstairs again, where the windows were larger, and she could more easily see her mother's approach.

But another hour passed, exhaustion tugging at Elizabeth's eyelids, and neither her mother nor her father returned. Elizabeth curled up in a ball on her chair, pulling her knees tight to her chest and sucking on her thumb to comfort herself as she waited, and waited. The sun was already rising by the time her father finally re-emerged. He walked with a stagger, and he had to pause for a moment outside the shop, his head down. Then he unlocked the door, and Elizabeth leapt to her feet.

"Where's mama?" she said

Her father shook his head and did not speak.

"Papa," she said. "Wasn't she at Mrs. Higgins's?"

"I don't know where she is, Elizabeth," her father said hoarsely. "There's no sign of her. I looked everywhere, but—"

"Then we have to tell the police!" Elizabeth said. She'd heard lots of stories where people got into trouble, and they all said that the police were the people to help. Her father and mother had taught her that too, while tucking her in at night, telling her that if she ever got lost or hurt and couldn't find her parents, then finding a policeman was the next best thing.

But her father shook his head again. "I've been," he said. "They wouldn't listen."

"What?" Elizabeth asked. That didn't make sense. She'd been taught that the police *always* helped.

Her father ran his hand through his hair. "They said we don't know she's really missing, that she might have just run off, and they can't waste time looking for a missing wife when she probably doesn't *want* to be found." Her father was murmuring almost to himself now. "But she would never run off like this," he said. "She must be in some sort of trouble. But I looked and I looked and—" He looked up suddenly, his eyes falling on Elizabeth again. "Have you seen any sign of her while I was gone? Did she say anything to you?"

Elizabeth shook her head.

"All right," her father said. "All right. Then—then I'd better look for her some more. Go upstairs, Elizabeth, and stay there. Don't open the door to anyone, you understand me?"

"But papa—".

"Go," he said, giving her a gentle push. "I'll be back as soon as I can."

But her father did not return for hours. The sun rose, and

Elizabeth sat upstairs with her face against the small window overlooking the street. Customers came to the still-locked door, confused that the store was not open, but her father did not return.

Then, around noon, two policemen walked to the front of the store and knocked.

Ignoring her father's warning, Elizabeth scurried down the stairs and unlocked the door. The policeman looked down at her. "Is your father home?" he asked.

Elizabeth shook her head.

"Is this the residence of Mrs. Lily Green?"

Elizabeth nodded, unable to speak.

"Your mother?" the second policeman asked her, not unkindly. She nodded again. The men glanced at one another, but before they could speak again, Elizabeth's father's voice cut through the street.

"Elizabeth!" he shouted. Elizabeth had never heard him speak so loudly before. She jumped and looked past the policemen to see her father running toward her.

"This is your father?" the first policeman asked her. She nodded as her father reached them and stepped around the policemen to put a hand on her shoulder.

"What's the problem, sirs?" her father asked. He looked pale, with dark circles under his eyes from lack of sleep.

"Mr. Samuel Green?" the first policeman asked. "I am afraid we have some bad news, sir. Perhaps—not in front of the child."

Elizabeth gripped hold of her father's arm. "Is it mama?" she asked, in a quiet voice. "What's happened to mama?"

"Elizabeth, go inside," her father said, but that only caused her to grip hold of his arm tighter. Her father glanced at her, and then all the fight seemed to drop out of him. "What happened?" he asked the policemen.

"She was found by the river this morning, sir," the policeman said.

7

Elizabeth felt a rush of joy. They'd found her mama! She would be coming home! But then she saw the way her father's face paled even further, and the grave expressions on the policemen's faces, and she thought perhaps she had misunderstood.

"What happened?" her father asked, his voice hoarse.

"We cannot say, sir. Got mixed up with something she shouldn't, most likely."

"No," her father said, shaking his head. "No, that's not her."

"These gangs," the policeman said, "they sometimes use pretty things like her to do their dirty work. Think they'll be able to get away with it easy, because they're women."

"No!" her father said again. "That is not what happened. She was not a criminal. Someone must have attacked her. It's murder."

"I am sorry, sir," the policeman said again. "We thought it best to inform you."

*Murder.* The word rang through Elizabeth's head. *Murder.* "Mama—mama's dead?" she asked, in a small voice.

Her father tightened his grip on her shoulder and then pushed her inside. "Go upstairs now, Elizabeth," he said. *"Now."*

He shouted so loudly that Elizabeth found herself obeying before she could think. The world spun around her as she climbed the stairs. None of it felt quite real. Her mama could not be dead. It didn't make any sense.

As soon as she was upstairs, she staggered back to her post by the window, where she could glimpse a little of the policemen's heads and hear some of the argument that drifted up from the street. Her father was shouting at the policemen, telling them that they had to find out who had done this, and the policemen were speaking sternly back to him, almost threatening him now that Elizabeth was gone. They told him if he did not stop arguing, they would investigate him and his business for criminal activity, too.

Elizabeth rested her head on her knees and sobbed.

# CHAPTER 2

The police did nothing to investigate the murder of Lily Green, and a heavy cloud of grief fell over Elizabeth and her father. Her father became prone to ranting about the corruption of the police at random moments of every day, insisting that Elizabeth stick to herself, and telling her to never, never go to them for help, not ever, because they could not be trusted not to betray you.

He also began speaking about perhaps leaving Birmingham and moving to a better place—perhaps London, he said—and through the pain of Elizabeth's grief, she felt a distant hint of excitement at the idea of seeing the capital. But after the expense of the funeral, they had no money to spare for any grand plans. Elizabeth took over her mother's role in the shop, and although her stitching was never quite as neat or as secure as her mother's had been, she worked as hard as she could, losing her grief in the gleam of the buttons and the steady rhythm of the sewing needle, and she improved day by day.

She missed her mother terribly, but she knew she must be watching over them both, and she desperately hoped she was making her proud.

One evening, a few months after her mother's disappearance, Elizabeth's father was tidying up the shop, while Elizabeth sat on a high stool, fixing a button to a frock, when the bell over the door rang. An unfamiliar man in a neat and crisp suit strode into the shop, a boy at his heels. The boy, Elizabeth thought, could only be a year or two older than she was, with a rather unruly mop of brown hair and freckles scattered across his nose. He did not look like the man's son, but he couldn't have been a servant either, because his clothes were far finer than anything Elizabeth had ever dreamt of wearing herself.

As Elizabeth considered them, waiting for her father to greet them, she realised that although the man was certainly a stranger, he wasn't as unfamiliar as she had originally thought. There was something about him that prodded at her memory. Then he looked directly at her, and she realised what it was. The man's dark eyes were exactly like her mother's had been.

"I'm sorry," her father said distractedly, as he turned to face the newcomers. "We're closing, but if it's only a quick request—" He broke off when he saw the man's face. "Elizabeth," he said, his tone immediately sterner. "Go upstairs."

"Papa?" she said.

"Now, Elizabeth."

Elizabeth put down the dress she was working on and hopped off the stool. She gave the stranger and the boy another curious glance as she walked to the stairs. The man smiled at her, and Elizabeth quickly looked away and ran up the stairs.

Elizabeth was generally an obedient child, trusting her father to know best. But her curiosity had been struck by the man's familiar eyes. Was it a coincidence, or was he connected with her mother somehow? She scrambled to the top of the stairs, but then she tucked herself around the corner, just out of sight, so that she could still listen to what the man might say.

"Who's the boy?" her papa asked coldly.

"This is my apprentice, Patrick," the man said.

Her father gave a low hum of disbelief but did not comment. "What do you want?" he asked the stranger.

"I'm here to see Elizabeth," the man said. "It's been years, Samuel."

"No," her papa said. "She will have nothing to do with you."

"Samuel, be reasonable—" the man said, but her father cut him off.

"She won't be involved in any of your business, Arthur. I suggest you leave."

Elizabeth could not resist. She peered around the corner at the top of the stairs for another glance at the man. He looked more disappointed than angry, she thought, and his entire appearance was richer than most of their customers ever looked. She couldn't imagine what terrible business such a man might be involved in, although it truly must be terrible for her father to respond to him so coldly.

The freckled boy looked up and spotted Elizabeth. She gasped, ready to duck away again, but then he winked at her and looked back at her father, saying nothing.

"Please, let me help you and your daughter," the man named Arthur said. "After what happened with Lily. I can give you money—"

"No," her papa said. "We do not want a penny from you. Good day to you, sir."

Arthur's face went blank, and silence hung between them. Then he nodded. "Good day, Samuel," he said. "Come along, Patrick."

And without another backward glance, the man strode out of the shop.

Elizabeth's father did not move for many long moments after the man had gone. He simply stared at the now-closed door. Elizabeth wished she could see the expression on her papa's face, but his back was to her. Then he sighed loudly and strode to the door to lock it.

Certain that the conversation was now over, Elizabeth crept the rest of the way to their living quarters.

Her father took longer than usual to finish tidying up the shop for closing, and Elizabeth considered climbing back down the stairs to help him several times, but something about her father's tone when he had seen the stranger kept her away. She had never heard her father speak so sharply to her, or so coldly to anyone. He would be very angry if he knew she'd stayed to listen.

Still, when he finally came upstairs, she could not stop herself from asking questions. "Who was that, papa?" she asked him.

"No one, Elizabeth," he said. "Forget him."

"But he seemed to know you—"

"I said forget him, Elizabeth," her father snapped. Elizabeth jumped, and her papa ran his hand through his hair, looking regretful. "I'm sorry, my dear," he said. "I didn't mean to shout. But he was no one. Now, why don't we see about supper?"

And Elizabeth was forced to let the subject drop.

# CHAPTER 3

*E*lizabeth did not mention the strange incident with the man and his apprentice again, and eventually it faded from her memory. A few years passed, and although Elizabeth was still heartbroken by her mother's death, the pain gradually became easier to bear. At thirteen, Elizabeth was tall for her age, with that new-born foal look of long arms and legs that the rest of her body had not quite yet grown to match. She and her father mostly kept to themselves, and were generally known around town as 'nice enough folk'—a little quiet, a little strange, but then Mr. Green had never really recovered from the shock of the death of his wife, and it must do strange things to a young girl, to be shut up in a shop all day with only her father for company.

Then a familiar-looking freckled-faced boy, a year or two older than her, walked into the button shop.

"Can I help you?" Elizabeth asked the boy, after he stepped through the doorway, sending the bell ringing, and looked somewhat nervously around.

"Um, yes," the boy said. He ran his hand nervously through his mop of brown hair, leaving parts of it standing on end. Elizabeth peered at him curiously, trying to remember where she had seen his face before. They had a lot of customers at the button shop, and the boy was certainly dressed well enough to be one, but customers did not usually enter the shop looking quite so uncertain, and something else about him was tugging at her memory, something she could not quite grasp.

"Have we met?" she asked him.

He nodded, once, and then coughed, clearing his throat. "Um, yes," he said. "We've met." She waited for a further explanation, and when several seconds passed without him speaking again, she prompted him.

"When?" she asked.

"Uh, a few years ago now, miss," the boy said. "I remember you, even if—even if you don't remember me. I'm an apprentice, miss. Came in with my master." He looked at her entreatingly again, as though urging her to remember.

"Your master?" she repeated."

"Mr. Arthur Taylor, miss," he said. "You, um—your father sent you upstairs, but you hid and listened in. I saw you and winked at you, miss. We were both a lot smaller then."

Elizabeth gaped at the boy as the memory rushed back to her. The well-dressed stranger, his eagerness to see her, her father's cold anger in response, and the young boy, a year or two older than she was, who he said was his apprentice.

"I remember," Elizabeth said quietly. Suddenly, she found she did not know what to do with her hands. She clasped them in front of her, but that felt too awkward, so she shook them out again, letting them hang by her sides. "What's your name?"

"Patrick, miss," he said.

"I'm Elizabeth," she said, and the boy named Patrick nodded.

"Is your father in, Miss Elizabeth?"

She shook her head, feeling suddenly nervous. Would he be angry if he found out she'd spoken to this boy? "He's out delivering an order," she said. "He, um—he should be back within an hour, though."

"Oh," Patrick said. He ran his hand through his hair again. "I'm expected back. I can't wait. But um—my master had a letter to deliver to him. Maybe you could take it?" He was already pulling an envelope out of his pocket as he spoke. He held it out toward Elizabeth, and Elizabeth took the few steps toward him to take it. Her fingers lightly brushed his as she took the envelope from his hands, and he jumped.

"Thank you," Elizabeth murmured. The envelope was surprisingly thick. Her father's name and address were both written on the front in cursive black ink. "But what—"

"I should really be going, miss," Patrick said. "Sorry to bother you. And thank you." He gave her an awkward nod, and then turned and strode out of the store.

For a wild moment, Elizabeth considered running after him, shouting for him to come back and answer her questions, but then the door closed behind him, and the noise was enough to jolt Elizabeth back to her senses.

She looked at the envelope in her hands. It was good quality paper, with a firm wax seal holding it closed. She ran her finger along the curling letters. Whoever had written the name and address obviously cared a lot about his correspondence. Had that been this Mr. Arthur Taylor? The man with her mother's eyes?

Elizabeth knew she should put the letter away somewhere safe and continue with her work, but it felt too heavy and important to put away. She put it in the pocket of her dress, reassured by the presence of its surprising weight, and returned to her sewing. Still, she found it hard to concentrate. Every thirty seconds or so, she found herself looking up at the door of the shop, hoping to see her father through the thick, smog-stained windows.

When he finally returned, an hour later, she leapt off her stool at once.

"Elizabeth!" her father said, sounding startled. "Is everything all right?"

"Yes, papa," Elizabeth said. "It's just—we had a visitor, while you were out. With a letter for you."

"A visitor?" her father asked mildly. "Must have been an interesting visitor if you're so excited. A big job, was it?"

Elizabeth approached her father and held out the letter. "It was a boy," she said. "An apprentice called Patrick. He left this for you." Her father took the letter and considered the elaborate writing with a frown. "He said it was from his master, a Mr. Arthur Taylor."

Upon hearing that name, her father's entire demeanour changed. His lips pressed tightly together in anger, and something like worry flashed in his eyes.

"His apprentice?" he repeated. "Not the man himself?"

"No, papa," Elizabeth said.

"What did his apprentice say?" her father asked sternly.

"Nothing much, papa," Elizabeth said, nerves now fluttering in her chest. "He just asked for you, and said he had a letter from his master, and said he was sorry to bother me, but he couldn't wait for you to return."

As she spoke, her father strode across the room, shaking his head. When he reached the fireplace, he tossed the letter into the ashes there. It was a warm spring day, with no need for any sort of fire, so the letter did not burn, but her father's intentions were still clear.

"Papa?" she asked softly.

"If that boy returns," her father said, "do not speak to him again. Fetch me at once."

"All right, papa," she said. She looked at the letter again, its pristine letters gleaming among the ash of the fireplace. "But— what if it's important?"

"Nothing that man has to say to us is worth listening to, Elizabeth, you hear me?" her papa said. He pressed a hand to his forehead and sighed. "Run along now. We need to finish Mrs. Lewis's order before day's end, and we won't get it done standing around talking like this."

Elizabeth nodded and returned quietly to her work, but she could not stop her gaze wandering back to the fireplace and the now soot-stained letter that lay there. Curiosity burned inside her. What could be so terrible about this man that her papa, usually so kind and warm-hearted to everyone, would refuse to even *open* his letter? Was he not at least curious why this man was writing to him? Perhaps her papa thought he already knew what the letter contained. But if that was the case, *what* exactly did he expect to be written inside it? Elizabeth struggled to focus on her work for the rest of that afternoon, and when she and her father locked up the shop and went upstairs for supper, she was so distracted that she almost burned their dinner.

Her father did not comment on her carelessness. He seemed lost in his own thoughts too, his lips pressed together with worry. He retired early, but Elizabeth found herself lying awake in bed for hours, staring up at the ceiling, her thoughts too loud to allow her to sleep. Who was this Mr. Arthur Taylor? What was in his letter that was so terrible that her father would not even open it?

If the next morning dawned cold, her father would light the fire downstairs, and the letter would be gone for good. She would never know what it said.

Maybe that was right, she thought. Her papa certainly did not want her to read it. He didn't seem to want *anyone* to read it. But the curiosity burned within her, keeping her awake no matter how much she tossed and turned. She had to know what the letter said.

One peek, she reasoned, would not be so terrible. She could look just long enough to satisfy her curiosity, to reassure herself that there was nothing all that interesting written in the letter at all, and then she would be able to sleep peacefully, and let it burn the next day without the slightest concern.

Elizabeth slipped out from under her bedclothes and tiptoed out through the apartment. She did not dare to light a candle upstairs, in case her father saw it, but the light of the full moon shone in through the window, illuminating the way.

She crept down the staircase into the shop. Her father had left a lantern burning on the desk, a careless mistake that she knew he would never normally make, proving just how distracted he had been by the letter. She left the lantern where it was and crept over to the fireplace.

Soot stained her hands as she picked up the envelope and considered the writing on it once more. As she walked back to the light of the lantern, she used her nails to break the seal. It split with a satisfying little crack, and she unfolded the envelope to reveal a small, simple letter on top of more bank notes than Elizabeth had ever seen in her life.

Hands shaking, she plucked the letter from the top of the pile and read it.

*This is for Elizabeth*, it read, in the same elaborate hand as had been on the envelope. *From her uncle.*

Elizabeth reread the note. It was only a few words, but they sent her stomach into knots, and she thought perhaps she might have misunderstood them. But as she read it a second and then a third time, she realised there was no mistake. *From her uncle.*

Was this Mr. Arthur Taylor her uncle? Or was he contacting her on behalf of her uncle? She did not know that she even had an uncle. As far as she knew, her father had been her only family ever since her mother died.

But then she remembered how it had struck her, when she saw that man several years before, how similar his eyes were to her mother's. Yes, she could believe the two of them were related. But for her mother to have a brother that her father had never once mentioned? A brother that he seemed desperate to keep away from Elizabeth at all costs, even if it meant burning an envelope full of money?

Elizabeth looked through the bank notes. She did not know much about money, and she rarely saw notes at all. They were white, with black printed writing on the front. The numbers seemed to leap out at her. *Five pounds. Five pounds. Ten pounds.* The shop earned them perhaps fifty pounds a year, and there had to be a hundred pounds here, tossed casually onto the fireplace like it meant nothing. Surely her father would not have planned to burn it if he had known.

But then Elizabeth remembered the cold anger in his face when he had met this man. Her uncle had offered money then as well, but her father had turned it down without a thought. What could her uncle possibly have done, she wondered, to make her father hate him this much?

She could not throw the money back into the fireplace, not now she had seen it. It would be beyond foolish to waste two years' worth of income based solely on prejudice or principle. She and her father could do many things with such an amount of money, and she knew that the world could be cruel. One day, they might find themselves in desperate need of it, and she thought perhaps her father would not be so opposed to it then, if it was the one thing that stood between their family and ruin.

She slipped the note back into the envelope and used the warmth from the lantern to soften the seal enough to fasten it again. It still looked like it had been opened, if anyone cared to look even vaguely closely, but Elizabeth imagined that her father would light the fire without giving it a second glance, just as he had tossed it away without much inspection or consideration the day before. She placed it back where it had landed in the hearth and crept back upstairs to hide the money under the floorboard beneath her bed, where, she hoped, her father would not look until they needed it.

# CHAPTER 4

*H*er father did not seem to notice anything was amiss when he rose the following morning. He lit the fire against the pre-dawn chill, and the letter from Elizabeth's uncle curled up and vanished in the flames.

He did not mention the letter or their visitor to Elizabeth again, and she did not mention the money in return. She found herself looking for the boy or his master every time the bell over the door rang, but neither of them returned, and although Elizabeth found herself looking at every face she passed when she was out on the street, checking for those familiar eyes, she saw no sign of either of them again.

She did not dare to spend the money. It seemed like a rebellion too far, and she felt guilty enough having read the letter in the first place, when her father had been so opposed to it. But money, she knew, was one of the most important things in this world, the thing that could decide one's happiness or ruin, and the day might well come when they would need it.

The letter and its fine handwriting was lost, but occasionally, when her father was out of the house on business, Elizabeth would pull the money out of its hiding place and think about the man with the elaborate handwriting who had sent it. Her mother's brother. What must he be like? Was he like her mother at all? Did he have fond memories of her, stories he could tell about her childhood that even Elizabeth's papa did not know? She did not think she would ever get to find out, but she liked to imagine it.

Elizabeth loved her papa, and she loved the button shop where they lived and worked, but as the years passed and she grew older, she began to chafe against the smallness of their world. Her father had no real social circle to speak of, and they were just well-to-do enough that it would be considered inappropriate for Elizabeth to introduce *herself* to anyone socially. Her father kept to himself, and he seemed to prefer the thought of Elizabeth always keeping to herself too, as though any contact with the world outside the shop might bring her mother's fate upon her, but Elizabeth dreamed of seeing what people and places the world had to offer outside of their tiny corner of it.

She tried to raise the subject of London with her father when she could. "There are so many opportunities there," she told him. "So many people! We could at least *visit.*"

But each time, her father just smiled somewhat sadly at her, and told her, "Maybe one day."

The years passed, and Elizabeth's questions about London came more and more frequently, but each time, her father would smile a little and say *one day, but not now.* Elizabeth desperately wanted to ask him when 'one day' might be, but she held her tongue. Still, she could not help herself dreaming of the big city, of a life where she was not quite so alone. She loved her father deeply, but she often found herself wondering what more the world might be.

Mr. Arthur Taylor and his apprentice did not return, but this time, Elizabeth could not forget them. The presence of the money beneath the floorboards ensured that. She had long since stopped hoping to see the boy's freckled face or her uncle's eyes every time the bell rang over the shop door, but she still had a distant hope that they would one day contact her and her father again. Perhaps, she thought, they already had. If Elizabeth was not present to witness it, her father certainly would not tell her about it.

By the time Elizabeth turned twenty, she was feeling increasingly trapped by life in the button shop. Her father still protected her like she was a child, refusing to allow her to form any real friendships with anyone her own age. Her father remained her whole world, and as wonderful as he was, that world was simply too small. Elizabeth wanted to make friends, perhaps even get married one day, and those things all required leaving home for more than simply walking to the market.

"Papa," she said, one summer evening, as they began to prepare the shop for closing. "Have you given any more thought to our going to London?"

Her father gave her that same sad smile as he shook his head. "Now isn't the best time, Elizabeth," he said. "But soon."

"Soon?" Elizabeth repeated. She found herself staring at him, anger bubbling up inside her, furious at that rueful smile he always had when she mentioned leaving. "Papa, you've been telling me *soon* for the past six years. *When* is soon?"

"Soon is soon, Elizabeth," her father said. "What do you expect from me? We don't have the money or the means to get to London. *Soon* means when we are able to."

"We could have gone years ago," Elizabeth said, all her loneliness and frustration rushing out of her in a few desperate words. "We would have more than enough if you'd accepted that money from my uncle, like he wanted you to do. How many more times has he offered to help us, and had you turn him down?"

Her father stared at her. "How do you know about him?" he asked.

"I saw him, didn't I?" she said. "When he came to the shop when I was a little girl, and when his apprentice came the time after, and you threw his letter on the fire. That envelope was full of money, papa! More money than we see in two years. And you wanted to *burn* it."

"We will never accept a penny from that man," her father said. Then he scowled. "How do you know what was in that envelope?"

"I opened it," Elizabeth said, her voice shaking slightly. "I wanted to see who that man was, to upset you so much. And it's a good thing I did! A hundred pounds, papa. From my *uncle*. You never told me I have an uncle."

"You don't have an uncle," her father said. "That man is dangerous, Elizabeth. What did you do with the money?"

Elizabeth hesitated. "I kept it," she said. "In case we needed it."

"Elizabeth," her father said sternly. "Fetch it at once.

Elizabeth shook her head. "You can't burn it," she said. "We *need* it, papa. You said yourself!"

"We need nothing from that man," her father insisted. "Elizabeth. Fetch it. Now."

Elizabeth hesitated and opened her mouth to argue again, but before she could speak, the shop doorbell rang. Both she and her father jumped and turned to look at the entrance. Five men were entering the shop.

"My apologies," her father said. "I'm afraid we're closed. We were just about to lock up."

The men ignored his words. They slowly crossed the room, and Elizabeth took an involuntary step back. She quickly took in the appearance of the men. They were of mixed age, from their twenties to their fifties, some clean-shaved, some hiding their faces behind beards. Their clothes were good quality, she saw at once, but they had been darned and mended beyond what Elizabeth thought a truly rich person would consider acceptable.

"I'm afraid you're going to have to come back tomorrow," her father said to the closest man. The man just smiled at him thinly. He stepped closer to her father and looked him up and down. Then, without warning, he punched her father in the stomach.

Her father let out a groan of pain as Elizabeth screamed. Another punch, and her father fell to the ground.

"Elizabeth," her father gasped, as the man's boot connected with his side. "*Run, Elizabeth.*"

Elizabeth could not run. She could not leave her father to the mercy of these men. But she was trembling from head to foot, completely unable to fight them. "Elizabeth!" her father shouted again, and the desperation in his voice was enough to overrule her own better instincts. She turned and fled as she heard another low thump and another groan of pain from her father.

"Fetch the girl," one of the men said calmly, as Elizabeth stumbled up the stairs.

"*No,*" she heard her father groan, as slow and steady footsteps began to follow her.

Elizabeth immediately realised her mistake. Yes, the men had been between her and the front door, but by running upstairs, she had only trapped herself further. Her mind went blank with terror as she heard her father shout again. *Get out,* she told herself, the thought racing through her head. *Just get out.*

The footsteps continued to make their way up the stairs behind her, and their steady pace was somehow far more frightening than if the man had been running. He truly thought she had no means of escape. Elizabeth looked around the room frantically, and her eyes fell on the window. It was fairly small, but, she thought, she might just be able to squeeze herself through. The man certainly would not be able to follow.

She ran over to it and threw open the shutters before looking at the drop. It was ten feet at least, down onto the stone alleyway behind the shop. But the footsteps continued to follow her, so she squeezed her way through the narrow opening, her sides scratching against the window frame as she pulled her head and shoulders through. She turned, gripping the stone with her fingers, just in time to see one of the men emerge at the top of the stairs. He leapt after her with a shout, but she was already moving again, clinging to the metal pipe that ran down the side of the house like it was her salvation. It creaked under her weight, but she did not plan to stick around long enough to see whether it would fall. She was already scrambling down the pipe as quickly as she could.

The man stuck his head out of the window above her and shouted, but she was already out of reach.

As soon as her feet touched the ground, she turned and ran again. She could smell smoke on the air. When she reached the end of the alley, she looked back over her shoulder.

Smoke was beginning to billow from the direction of her home. Elizabeth swayed on the spot. Her *father*.

For a desperate moment, she considered going to the police for help. But her father had always told her that the police in Birmingham were useless and corrupt, unwilling to help people like them unless they put a significant amount of money on the table. *We have to take care of ourselves, Elizabeth,* he told her, *and that means keeping to ourselves and staying out of trouble.*

But that hadn't helped them in the end. Who were those men? She was certain she'd never seen them before in her life, and based on her father's initial reaction to them, she didn't think he knew them either. But they had attacked him without word or explanation, as though they expected him to already know the message they were sending.

Unless the message was intended for someone else. But who could it be, when they had no friends or relatives to speak of?

Her heartrate quickened again as she imagined the men coming into the alley behind the shop in search of her. What would they do if they found her? She couldn't leave her papa to suffer, but if she stayed… if she stayed…

Movement at the opposite end of the alley was enough to send her running again. She raced around the corner, diving blindly through the streets, not daring to look back even once to see if anyone was following her.

When she finally stopped to catch her breath again, she did not recognise any of the buildings around her. She was on a narrow backstreet of some kind, but it was not one she'd ever walked before. She wrapped her arms around herself, fighting back a shiver, as tears formed in her eyes. But did it matter that she was lost, if she had no one to go to? No friends, no relatives, not even neighbours who cared enough to help. She'd run out in her dress and boots, without even a bonnet for her head or a cloak to warm her, without a single penny in her pockets. She thought of the money hidden under the floorboard, the gift from her supposed uncle, and let out another sob. She should have taken the time to grab it. Then she might have been able to persuade *someone* to help them. Maybe she could even have used it to pay the thugs to leave.

She pressed her hands over her face and took a long, steadying breath. She could not have gone for the money, she told herself. Any further hesitation and she would have been caught. There would have been nothing to stop the thugs taking the money and still attacking her and her father both, and if they had seen her fleeing with a handful of banknotes, they would not have given up the chase so easily.

She took another deep breath, trying to think. Who could possibly help them? The only name that came to mind was this uncle, this Arthur Taylor. He had said he wanted to help Elizabeth and her father, hadn't he? But Elizabeth knew nothing about him beyond his name. He might not even live in Birmingham at all. And Taylor was hardly an uncommon surname. There could be tens of Arthur Taylors in this one city alone.

No, she would have to face this problem herself. The sun was beginning to set, casting the city in the hazy grey light of a late summer evening, twilight that would stretch on for at least an hour or two yet. Were the men still at the store? Was her father looking for her? She wiped her tears from her eyes with the back of her hand and nodded resolutely to herself. She had to go back home, to see what had happened. If she hid in the shadows, she would be able to watch unseen, and make sure the men were gone before she got too close.

The journey home took far longer than her sprint through the streets. She had to study every street sign and shop window, searching for clues about her location, and once she figured out where she was, she had a good half an hour walk left through the emptying city streets before she reached their street.

The stench of smoke hung heavy in the air as she approached their street. Her stomach sinking, already knowing what she was going to find, Elizabeth crept down the darkening street to the shop's front door.

There was nothing left. Their business, their home, was nothing but a smouldering, burned-out husk.

# CHAPTER 5

*E*lizabeth scrambled through the soot and ash, looking
for any sign of the men or of her father. A little blood
splattered the ground near where the counter had been, but no
matter how desperately she searched, she could not find any
hint about her father. Had the men grabbed him and dragged
him elsewhere? But what would have been the purpose in that?
She and her father had no money to pay a ransom, no connec-
tions that might care about his absence.

No, if the men had dragged her father away, it was to hide
what they had done from anyone who might investigate. Elizabeth sat down in the ashes, her breaths coming in frantic gasps.
Her father could not afford a hospital. If he wasn't here... he
had to be dead.

Elizabeth let out a sob, and then pressed her hands over her
mouth, fighting the urge to scream. The thugs might yet return
looking for her. She could not give herself away. But her entire
body was trembling, her head spinning from the shock of her
discovery and the thick smell of soot.

Once again, she considered going to the police. And once

again, terror struck her at the thought. Her father had always insisted that she should never get the police involved, not *ever*. They had not helped her mama when she had needed it. They would only take advantage of her if she asked for their help.

She needed to breathe. She needed to think.

She looked over at the stairway, wondering whether she might climb upstairs and search for the money, but the wooden steps were broken and charred, and she doubted they would hold her weight. Even if they would, the ceiling was black and collapsed in places. The bank notes were surely burnt into ash.

She could not stay here. Her hands and legs trembled, but she forced herself to stand and brush what ash she could from her dress. She needed to focus on her next step. Just her very next step. Other worries could come later. She needed to leave and find somewhere to rest before it got completely dark. That was all she could worry about right now.

Elizabeth ended up sleeping in an alley behind a bakery, about an hour's walk away from the store. The alley was unlit, but it was unoccupied too, and she leant back against the bakery wall and closed her eyes, exhaustion pulling at her. The air was a little chilly, but she was thankful that it was summer, and the temperature was merely uncomfortable, not dangerous. Still, she wished she had a cloak with her. She folded her knees up to her chest, burying her hands under her skirts, and slept.

The rising sun woke her early the following morning. For a moment, Elizabeth did not know where she was. She felt the hard ground beneath her and the wall at her back, and she jerked awake, her heart racing. She blinked blearily at the alley, gently lit by the pre-dawn light, and then her heart and stomach both sank as the events of the previous day came back to her.

Her father was dead. He was dead, and she had no home to go to, no friends to help her, absolutely nothing but the soot-covered clothes on her back. She pulled her legs in tighter against her face and hid her face in her knees, but then jumped when she heard the sound of movement in the bakery behind her. The baker must have risen early to prepare for the day. Elizabeth did not know what he would do if he found her sleeping here, but she could not imagine it would be kind. She got quickly to her feet and hurried away.

She spent the morning wandering the streets of Birmingham, desperately trying to think of somewhere to turn. People took one look at her ragged, soot-covered appearance and gave her a wide berth, and Elizabeth could not blame them. She felt broken and lost, but what could she do, and where could she go, other than the workhouse?

No, she thought. She was not so desperate as that just yet. But her stomach was beginning to ache with hunger, and she wondered how long she would last without any money. She looked too bedraggled to convince any shop she passed to hire her, but she did not have money to use the public baths. She would not get far if she did not eat, but unless she searched in the bins for food, she would be forced to steal some, and she knew that her father would never approve. If it made the difference between starving and surviving, then perhaps she might be able to justify it, but even so, stealing was a sin, and how could she know that whoever she stole from would not suffer themselves because of her actions? And that was not even considering the very real possibility that she might be caught.

By mid-afternoon, she felt dizzy from hunger and exhaustion, and she found herself sneaking into the back alleys again, hoping perhaps to find some burnt bread or abandoned crumbs to eat.

"Hello there, miss."

Elizabeth jumped and spun around. A stranger had approached her without her noticing. He was a well-dressed man, seemingly in his forties, his neat brown hair and beard lightly specked with grey. His eyes flicked up and down Elizabeth, taking in her dishevelled appearance, and a predatory smile spread across his lips. Elizabeth took an unintentional step back.

"You're looking a bit hungry there, miss, if you don't mind my saying so. Fallen on some rough times, have you?"

Elizabeth did not reply. She clenched her hand into a fist at her side to hide the way it shook. She did not like the hungry way the man was looking at her, not one bit.

"You're a pretty little thing," he said, "under that dust and dirt there. No need to go hungry now is there, when you're as lovely looking as you?"

"I don't know what you are implying, sir," Elizabeth said, raising her chin in defiance as she glared back at him.

"Of course, you do," he said. "But I'm not implying anything. I'm asking. A girl like you could make some good money with the right direction. I got some other girls that could help teach you. Then you wouldn't have to be hungry. You could have everything you wanted."

"No, thank you, sir," Elizabeth said. She took another involuntary step back.

He sneered at her. "You think you're likely to get a better offer, girl?"

"I don't want any offer," Elizabeth said. "I'm not a—a—" She stumbled over her words, and the man grinned.

"Don't look down on the business, girl. It'll be your bread and butter soon enough. You mark my words. Now why don't you come with me, and I'll show you how to get started." He reached forward and tried to grab Elizabeth's wrist, and she jumped and pulled it away.

"Leave me alone," she shouted, her voice shaking. The man reached for her again, and this time he seized her upper arm, his fingers digging in hard enough to bruise.

"I *said*, you're coming with me," he said, and he began to drag her down the alley.

"No!" Elizabeth shouted. Her feet scrambled for purchase on the ground, and she struggled against him, but he pulled her along as though she weighed nothing. "Stop!"

She kicked the man hard on the shin, and he swore and let go of her. His moment of distraction was enough. Elizabeth turned and ran down the alley, her hair streaming behind her.

"You little—" the man shouted. "Come here!" She could hear his footsteps pounding on the ground behind her. Elizabeth squeezed her eyes shut, urging her legs to move faster, but she knew the man was much taller than her, and she could not outrun him for long.

She skidded around the corner, hoping to emerge onto a main street, but it was another alley. She kept running, the air burning in her lungs, knowing that at any moment the man would reach her, he would capture her, he would punish her for fighting back....

"Oi!" Elizabeth jumped as another man stumbled into the alley in front of her. Where the first stranger had been neat and well-dressed, this man was unkempt, with a wild, filthy beard and torn clothes covered in dirt. His eyes rolled as he looked past Elizabeth at the man chasing her. "Oi, you there," he said, his words slurring together. "You there. Got a penny to spare?"

He lurched forward, putting himself between Elizabeth and the other man. Elizabeth urged herself to keep running. She raced around another corner, to find herself faced with a dead end. Gasping for breath, she turned. The new stranger was still stumbling toward her pursuer with his arms outstretched.

"One a penny, two a penny, hot cross buns," the man sang, the words slurring together. "If you've no daughters, give 'em to your sons. Well, I used to have a daughter, I did, but we never had any pennies for buns, and she's gone now. Gone far, far away." The man lurched forward and rested a hand on Elizabeth's pursuer's shoulder. He flinched back, looking at the singing beggar with a mixture of horror and disgust.

"Got a penny? Just a penny?" the man said. He began to sing again as his hand shook the other man's shoulder. "If you've no kind of pretty elves, eat 'em all yourself!"

Elizabeth's pursuer shoved the beggar away. "Get off me," he spat. "Don't touch me."

"No penny for a beggar, sir?" the beggar asked, reaching for him again. "All my pennies left me. All my family too. Have pity for a poor old beggar, eh?"

Elizabeth's pursuer scoffed. He shoved the beggar back, and then turned on his heel and strode away, wiping the dirt from his shoulder as he went.

The beggar watched him leave, half chanting and half singing the words "hot cross buns" to himself, but once the other man had disappeared around the corner, he straightened up and stopped singing at once.

"You all right there, miss?" he said, his voice far more coherent now. "He didn't hurt you, did he?"

Elizabeth's hands shook, but she was stuck in a dead end, with nowhere else to run, and despite the man's appearance, it seemed that he had just rescued her. "I'm not hurt," she said softly, as she stepped back into the alley. "He wanted to, but—"

"I see sorts like that every day," the beggar said. "Worst kind of folk. I'm a beggar, me, and I look like one. It might be illegal, but I make no pretences. Men like that, dressing up in fine clothes, using young girls in need of help to pay for them—it's foul, if you ask me. But glad to hear you're all right, miss."

Elizabeth stepped closer. The stranger had a wild beard and hair, but his expression was soft, and he had a kind glint in his eye.

"The name's Joey, miss," he said. He did not hold out a hand for Elizabeth to shake, but he nodded his head slightly, and Elizabeth nodded in return.

"I'm Elizabeth," she said.

"Well, Elizabeth," he said. "I s'pose there's nothing gained in asking you how you ended up here, is there? Everyone's got a story, and none of 'em are good. But you look like you've been through more'n most over the past few days. You new on the streets? You got anywhere to go?"

"No," Elizabeth said, her voice shaking. "I mean, yes, I lost my home yesterday in—in a fire. And no, I have nowhere to go. My papa, he—" A sob burst out of her, cutting off her words. She rubbed her eyes with her hand, feeling foolish. "I'm sorry," she said.

"No need to be sorry," Joey said. "It's hard. I know. When I lost my daughter, I—well." He swallowed. "No use dragging up the past now, is there? We've got enough to keep us busy in the present. You've got nowhere to go. And I hate to admit it, lass, but there will be more men like that one around these streets as it gets dark. Might be, once you get hungry enough, you won't be able to refuse 'em."

"I could go to the workhouse," Elizabeth said softly, but Joey shook his head.

"Not if you can help it," he said. "That place crushes the soul outta ya. Believe me. Better dead than in there. It ain't no real life. But if you wander around much longer, I hate to think what might happen to you either. Birmingham's got some bad people in it, probably more bad than good."

"I know," Elizabeth said. "I found that out last night."

Joey considered her for a moment. "I don't have much," he said, "but I got a place to shelter, and that's something. Now I know you don't know me, Miss Elizabeth, but you'd be safe wi' me, at least til you figure out what you're gonna do."

He kept a respectful distance and simply looked at her patiently while she considered his offer. Elizabeth could not deny that he was a little frightening, just based on his appearance and his status as a stranger, but he had a gentle look in his eyes, and he had just rescued her, when he could just have easily left her to her fate. She was not certain she could trust him—

*why* was he helping her?—but she couldn't deny that she needed some assistance, before some other person with ill intentions came across her.

"All right," she said. "Yes, thank you."

"Excellent," the man said. He nodded to her and began to walk back the way he had come. "Follow me, then."

# CHAPTER 6

*J*oey lived in a small hovel down a side alley, constructed out of pieces of old wooden crates and cardboard propped against the wall. Joey settled down on a nest of tattered blankets and picked up one to pass to Elizabeth. It was thin and somewhat dirty, but Elizabeth wrapped it around her shoulders nonetheless, and was immediately grateful for its extra warmth.

"Here," he said, pulling a small loaf of bread from his pocket. "It's not much, but what's mine is yours." He split it into two pieces and handed Elizabeth half. She was too hungry to refuse. The bread was a little stale, but after not eating anything for over a day, Elizabeth found it delicious. She ate it all in four bites, and then licked the crumbs from her fingers.

"Thank you," she whispered, once she was done.

"No problem," Joey said. He sighed and leaned back against the wall, closing his eyes. "It's good to have some company," he said. "Been alone for too long. No one wants to talk to a filthy beggar like me. Still, it's useful sometimes, eh? Scared that boy away fast enough."

"Have you always been homeless?" Elizabeth asked softly.

Joey shook his head. "No," he said. "No, I used to live well enough. But Birmingham is dangerous, like I said. I was a carpenter, you know. Had my own shop. But it was attacked by a criminal gang. I don't know why. I never had nothing to do with any gang, but they must've had their reasons, mustn't they? Destroyed the shop, left me penniless, lost me my little girl. And now I live here."

"I'm sorry," Elizabeth said softly.

"Nothing to be done about it," Joey murmured.

Elizabeth wrapped her arms around her knees and stared at the wall, memories of the gang flooding back. "I think that's what happened to me," she said. "I don't know, but—some men came into my father's shop and started beating him. I wanted to help, but—" She swallowed a sob. "There was nothing I could do. He told me to run, and there was nothing I could do—"

"Hey, now, miss," Joey said kindly. "You did the right thing. Your father would've wanted you to get out okay. I've always thought, if my little girl could have survived instead of me… your pa will've been glad you escaped."

"But I just left him," she said. "I just *ran*. And when I came back, they'd burned down the shop, and my father was gone."

"He might've gotten out," Joey said, but he did not sound particularly convinced of it, and Elizabeth shook her head.

"He would've found me if he was alive and able," she said. "And they wouldn't take him alive. There's no one who would offer anything for us. He must be dead. He died, and then they took him, to hide him—" She gasped and pressed her hands over her mouth to hold back her sob.

"Hey, it's all right now," Joey said. "You're safe."

"You told me Birmingham was dangerous," she said, in a quiet voice, sniffing slightly.

"Ay, that I did," he said. "And that'd be the truth. It's dangerous out there, and a young girl like you should be careful.

It's why I asked you to come here. You shouldn't have to be alone."

"Thank you," Elizabeth said, and Joey nodded.

"Well," he said. "I'm beat, that's for certain. Try and get some sleep, girl. It'll do you good."

Elizabeth nodded, but Joey had already closed his eyes again, so she settled her head back against the wall, and tried to rest. She expected it to be difficult to sleep, after all she had gone through, but although she still felt a little afraid of Joey, she found that she nodded off quickly and slept far better than she had the night before with the blanket and makeshift walls to keep her warm.

When she awoke, Joey was already up, as was the sun. "Sleep well?" he asked her, when he saw she was awake. "Sun's been up a couple of hours, but I thought I should let you rest. You looked like you needed it."

"Thank you," Elizabeth said. She stretched out the stiffness in her shoulder, trying not to think about what the day might bring. "You've been very kind to me."

"It's nothing," Joey said. "A man needs someone to talk to every now and then, don't you think, or he really will go crazy. So really, I should be thanking you." He gave her a careful look. "Now, I don't know what you plan to do for food today, but if it don't offend you too much, you could come sit begging with me. Should make enough to buy some supper, at least, and I don't think it's much of a crime, as long as people are willing to give it to you. Gotta keep an eye out for the police though."

"Yes, of course," Elizabeth said. Two days ago, she would never have imagined that she would be begging on the streets, but the hunger in her stomach was too insistent to ignore. At least if people gave her money out of pity, she could be certain that she wasn't taking anything that they were unable to spare.

She and Joey settled on the edge of a busy shopping street, Joey's hat cast in front of them for coins. Elizabeth wished she could get some of the dirt off her dress and her skin, certain that everyone would look at her with disgust, but most of the looks she received were more pity than horror. She did not realise how innocent she looked, her blonde curls stained with soot, her large eyes filled with sadness, but passers-by noticed, and they began to toss coins into Joey's hat.

"For you and your daughter," one woman said, smiling at the pair with pity, and although the word broke Elizabeth's heart, she did not correct her.

"You're a lucky charm," Joey said, after they had passed a few hours on the street and gathered a couple of shillings worth of donations. "I've never received so much in all my begging life."

Elizabeth looked at the few dirty coins sitting in his hat. They did not look like much to her. But Joey seemed thrilled.

"We're doing well?" she asked him, a little hesitantly.

"It's been a long time since I've seen this much," Joey said. When no one was looking, he plucked a few coins from the hat and tucked them into his pocket. "Can't have people thinking we're doing *too* well, though," he said to Elizabeth with a wink. "They need to think they're saving us from starvation, or they won't give us a penny."

Elizabeth nodded and fidgeted, sore from sitting for so long on the ground. She looked over the crowd, wishing she might see a familiar face, but knowing there were no familiar faces to see. Her father would certainly not be among them.

Then she froze as her eyes fell on a somewhat familiar young man. It took her a moment to place him, and then, when she did, she gasped. It was Patrick, the apprentice who had brought the letter and the money all those years ago. He was older than the last time she had seen him, in his early twenties now, but he still had the same slightly messy brown hair and freckles across his face. But any childishness that had remained in his appearance was now gone, replaced by a tall, strong-looking young man with handsome features beneath his freckles and a serious expression on his face.

As though sensing her gaze, the man who looked like Patrick stopped and turned, his eyes falling on her. She blushed instantly, knowing she must look truly wild, so rough and unkempt compared to the fineness of his clothes. For a moment, their eyes met. Elizabeth thought she saw a spark of recognition there, but she must have imagined it, because a moment later, he was turning away and disappearing into the crowd.

Elizabeth looked down at her hands in her lap, feeling her face burning. She had soot stuck under her fingernails, and her skin looked cracked and raw. No wonder he had walked away from her. Even if he had recognised her—and why would he, when they had met twice, years and years ago?—he would want nothing to do with a beggar girl like her.

And who was to say it even was Patrick? It had been years since she had seen him. She might have just conjured the figure out of her imagination, out of desperation, pinning his identity onto any passing brown-haired young man, or dreaming him out of thin air entirely.

She rubbed her arms with her hands to fend off the chill that struck her. She felt even lonelier now her mind had played such a cruel trick on her.

But she wasn't completely alone, she told herself, with a sideways glance at Joey. She had an ally. Maybe even a friend. She did not know him all that well, but he had saved her when she desperately needed saving, and now together they were earning their supper. That was far more than she had had twenty-four hours before.

"Elizabeth?" an unfamiliar voice asked. She looked up again, and almost jumped. A tall, well-dressed man in his forties or fifties stood before her, beaming. He had a good-natured face, with a slightly crooked nose and ruddy cheeks, but the thing that drew Elizabeth's attention most was his eyes. She had not seen her mother's eyes for thirteen years now, but she still felt a pang of recognition deep in her heart when she looked up at the stranger. He had her mother's eyes.

"Elizabeth?" he said again. "Is that you?"

She nodded, scrambling to her feet. "Yes," she said. "Are you —Mr. Taylor?"

"Arthur Taylor," he said. "Your Uncle Arthur. You look just like your mother, Elizabeth, truly you do. It's like a vision from the past."

Joey remained seated beside her. Elizabeth attempted to brush some of the soot from her skirt.

The freckled young man she had seen before stood beside Mr. Taylor, smiling tentatively at her too.

"Patrick was the one who spotted you," Mr. Taylor said. "He said he was certain you were the girl he met in the button factory those years ago. And one look at you was enough to tell me the truth of it. Perhaps your father never mentioned me. I was your mother's older brother. What happened? Where's your father?"

Elizabeth felt a sob rising in her throat, and Mr. Taylor must have noticed it, for he quickly shook his head. "Later," he said. "We can talk about it later. First, let's get you fed and cleaned up."

Elizabeth hesitated. This man was basically a stranger to her, and her father had been insistent that she never accept any help from him or even meet him at all. But her father was dead, and Elizabeth had nothing except Joey's friendship, bought out of pity. What would happen when he got tired of her being a burden on him? And she had wished for a familiar face, hadn't she? She had wondered where Arthur Taylor might be. Her wish had been granted. She would be foolish to turn her back on that.

"All right," she said softly. She turned to Joey, who still sat on the ground beside her. "Thank you so much for helping me,

Joey," she said. "You saved me, really you did." Joey nodded, but there was a wariness in his eyes that she had not seen before. He glanced at Arthur and then back to Elizabeth.

"That's all right, Miss Elizabeth," he said in a rough voice. He pulled some coins from the hat and held them out to her, but she shook her head.

"Please, keep all the money," she said. "You've more than earned it."

"No, miss," he said. He pressed a few coins into her hand. "You keep some. Just in case you find you need it." He glanced at Arthur again and then looked at the ground. Elizabeth was about to ask him if they knew each other, when Arthur clapped a hand on her shoulder.

"Come along," he said. "Let's get you something to eat."

# CHAPTER 7

*E*lizabeth was grateful when her Uncle Arthur gave her his coat to wrap around herself as they walked. She felt humiliated that he had seen her in such a state, and even more embarrassed when she thought of Patrick, with his handsome face and fine clothes, seeing her covered in soot and grime. She was as eager to cover herself as Uncle Arthur must have been to avoid being seen with such a rough-looking girl.

"Thank you," she said again as they walked. "I know we don't really know each other, but—"

"You're family," Uncle Arthur said. "I wanted to meet you long ago. Any help I can give is an honour."

"You're probably wondering what happened—" Elizabeth began, but he shushed her.

"No need to go into it now," he said. "Let's see you safe and warm first. Then we can talk about the particulars."

Uncle Arthur led her out of central Birmingham onto a street of well-to-do-looking town houses, and Elizabeth pulled the coat tighter around herself as they passed a man in a top hat who nodded in greeting to her uncle.

They stopped outside one of the largest houses on the street, with a shiny iron fence and a front door painted black. As Uncle Arthur led her up the front path, the door opened, revealing a short, grey-haired woman with soft brown eyes.

"Ah, Miss Dawn," Uncle Arthur said. "Turns out Patrick wasn't mistaken. This here is my niece, Elizabeth. Lily's girl."

"A pleasure to meet you, dear," Miss Dawn said, with a slight curtsey and a far bigger smile. "I knew your mother when she was a lass. You look just like her."

"Thank you," Elizabeth whispered. She did not know what else to say.

"Oh, you poor dear," Miss Dawn said, when she got a closer look at her. "What have you been through? Come on with me, now. Give me a moment to run you a hot bath, and then we'll get you into some clean clothes." She put her arms around Elizabeth and began to lead her toward the stairs. Elizabeth glanced back at Uncle Arthur, and he smiled and nodded encouragingly at her.

"You're in good hands with Miss Dawn," he said. "Don't worry about a thing."

Elizabeth nodded, unable to speak. The house they had entered must be twice the size of the shop and their apartment combined. The dark wooden floor gleamed, and the walls were covered in elaborate paper decorated with green vines. Elizabeth expected to be led to the kitchen, where water might be heated for the bathtub, but Miss Dawn guided her up the stairs instead.

She led her into a room that seemed to have been built for the sole purpose of washing, with a large bathtub and a porcelain sink beneath two metal taps. Elizabeth's home had running water too, so the taps were not a complete surprise, but Elizabeth still could not help but gape when Miss Dawn turned one on over the bath and steaming hot water rushed out.

"Good, isn't it?" Miss Dawn said, noticing the expression on

Elizabeth's face. "I don't understand how it all works myself, but the master had it installed a few years back. The range heats the water downstairs, and then it's stored until you want to use it. No need to wait for the kettle over the fire for your bath."

Elizabeth gaped at the hot water as Miss Dawn gently removed Uncle Arthur's coat from around her shoulders and then began to help her to undress. Elizabeth was too surprised and too exhausted to feel embarrassed. She leaned into this kindly woman's help and allowed her to guide her into the bathtub and begin scrubbing her with a brush and soap. The movement brought back memories of her mother, giving her a bath in the kitchen in front of the fire, and she closed her eyes to prevent any tears from falling. The heat of the water was soothing, at least, easing some of the tension from her muscles. The water turned black around her as Miss Dawn cleaned the dirt and soot from Elizabeth's hands and arms, and then used a cup of water to rinse through Elizabeth's hair.

Miss Dawn left the room for a moment but returned soon afterward with a pile of clothes in her arms. "These should fit you," she said. "They're a bit old now, certainly not fashionable anymore, but they're clean and warm. They belonged to your mother before she got married, and they've been sitting in a trunk ever since."

"My mama used to live *here?*" Elizabeth asked. This was by far the finest house she had ever seen. If she had not been so heartbroken and exhausted, she thought she would have been embarrassed to be inside it, desperately aware of how little she belonged. Had her mother really once lived in this place, before moving to the button shop with her father?

"Oh, yes," Miss Dawn said. She helped Elizabeth out of the tub and gently towelled her dry, before helping her to dress in her mother's clothes. Her mother must have been a little taller than Elizabeth, because the dress was slightly too long, but it fit well enough.

Miss Dawn towelled off Elizabeth's hair too and then braided it up to dry. "There we are," she said. "You look lovely, dear. Just like your mother used to."

"Thank you," Elizabeth said softly. She found it difficult to speak, but she hoped her deep appreciation was clear in her words, nonetheless. Miss Dawn smiled at her like she understood.

"Come on, now," she said. "Let's get some food into you. That will perk you right up, I bet. And I think your uncle wanted to talk to you, once you felt a bit more human again."

Elizabeth followed Miss Dawn out of the bathroom and back down the stairs. Once again, she expected to be led into the kitchen, but instead Miss Dawn led her into a room that's only purpose seemed to be for eating. A large oak table surrounded by high-backed chairs took up much of the space, and there was an ornate mantelpiece over a large, currently unlit fireplace. Uncle Arthur and Patrick both sat around the table, which was covered with an array of cold meats, bread and vegetables.

"There you are," Uncle Arthur said. "Are you feeling better?"

"Yes, thank you," Elizabeth said. Miss Dawn ushered her to one of the chairs, and she carefully sat down. Miss Dawn smiled at Elizabeth, curtsied to Uncle Arthur, and left the room. Elizabeth had to resist the urge to call after her and ask her to stay. The older woman's presence was warm and reassuring, and Elizabeth immediately missed it as she turned to look at the unfamiliar man who was her uncle.

"Eat anything you like," he said. "As much as you like." When she didn't move, he leaned forward and began to pile food onto a plate for her. Elizabeth stomach ached with hunger, but she did not think she could eat a bite while she still felt so uncertain. Uncle Arthur passed the plate to Patrick, and the boy put it in front of Elizabeth with a smile, but she could not bring herself to smile back.

"Now, please, Elizabeth. If you can. Tell me what happened."

"Strange men came into the button shop," she said, her voice shaking slightly. "I didn't recognise any of them, and I don't think papa did either, but—they attacked him. They didn't even say anything to him or threaten him. They just attacked him. My papa told me to run. I didn't want to, but—" She broke off and closed her eyes.

"You did the right thing, Elizabeth," her uncle said gently. "They sound like they were dangerous men."

Elizabeth nodded, steeling herself to speak again. "They burned down the store," she said. "I ran as far as I could, and when I came back, the store was burned away, and there was no sign of my father. I think—I think he must be dead."

Uncle Arthur closed his eyes, as though in resignation, and bowed his head. "It grieves me to hear that," he said. "Samuel was a good man. I know your mother loved him very dearly."

"But why would anyone want to hurt him?" Elizabeth said. "I don't think they even robbed us. They just attacked him. He didn't have any enemies. We barely knew anybody. Why did this happen?"

"I don't know, child," Uncle Arthur said. "This city can be a dangerous place. It may have been a purely random attack. There are many criminals in this city looking to build their reputation, to prove how strong and dangerous they are to the men around them. I am not sure that anything could have prevented it or warned you of it before it happened. Some people are just wicked."

"Is that what happened to my mama?" Elizabeth asked softly. "Did random criminals attack her?"

Uncle Arthur looked startled, but then his expression softened. "Did your father never talk to you about what happened to your mother?"

"No," Elizabeth said. "He never wanted to speak of it. But I overheard the police speaking with him. Someone killed her, and the police accused her of being involved in a criminal gang—"

"Your mother," Uncle Arthur interrupted firmly, "would never be involved in such a thing. She was the best person I knew."

"I didn't believe them," she said. "And papa didn't either. But the police wouldn't investigate what happened."

"No," Uncle Arthur said with a sigh. "Never trust the police here." He shook his head. "I don't know precisely what happened to your mother that night, but it seemed it was a random act of violence too. I am sorry that it has hurt you so deeply. I'm just thankful that Patrick found you when he did. You weren't hurt, were you, while you were on the street?"

"No," Elizabeth said. "There was one man. He chased me, but —the man I was with earlier, Joey, he frightened him away and helped me."

"Still," Uncle Arthur said, "I am glad we found you when we did. The only question, really, is what to do from here."

"Can't she stay here with us?" Patrick asked. Both Uncle Arthur and Elizabeth turned to look at him, and he blushed beneath his freckles as he realised how eager he had sounded. Elizabeth found herself blushing too, that this kind-seeming and handsome young man seemed so keen for her to stay. Patrick coughed awkwardly. "Sorry," he said. "I only meant—"

"Of course, Elizabeth is welcome to stay here, if that's what she wishes," Arthur said with a smile. "What do you think, Elizabeth? If my overeager apprentice has not put you off."

"No, sir," she said, with a small, self-conscious smile. "If you truly don't mind, I—I would really appreciate it if I could stay with you."

"Wonderful!" Uncle Arthur said, clapping his hands together. Patrick grinned too, although he was staring at his plate, apparently unable to risk looking Elizabeth in the eyes. "I'm truly sorry for what has happened to you, Elizabeth, but I feel blessed that I finally have the opportunity to get to know you, and help you as I have wanted to ever since before we lost your mother. Please trust that you will be safe and well here."

And faced with his and Patrick's smiles and encouraging eyes, she could not help but trust him.

# CHAPTER 8

*M*iss Dawn showed Elizabeth to her mother's old bedroom, apologising for the slightly musty nature of the room. She told Elizabeth that it had become the guest bedroom since her mother got married—a bedroom *only* for guests to use? It was a luxury that Elizabeth could never have imagined—and she knew her mother would have loved to know that one day it would be Elizabeth's own.

Elizabeth thought that perhaps the excitement and terror of the past couple of days might keep her awake, but she passed out on the soft bed at once, and only awoke well after dawn. She felt a little embarrassed over her laziness as she quickly dressed, terrified of what her uncle might think of her, and when she hurried downstairs, she found that Uncle Arthur and Patrick had both already left for the day's work.

"What do they do?" Elizabeth asked Miss Dawn, as the older woman spooned hot porridge into a bowl for her and fussed over how well she had slept.

"Oh, the master owns some factory or other, down by the river," Miss Dawn said. "A family business."

"A factory making what?" Elizabeth asked.

"I've never fully understood that," Miss Dawn said. "Something to do with the trains. It's big business, isn't it, connecting the country together? But the *how* of it all is a bit beyond me, I'm afraid."

Once she had finished her breakfast, Elizabeth rose to wash the dishes, and Miss Dawn tried to bat her away. "Don't be doing that, now," she said. "That's my job."

"I want to be useful," she said. "Surely there's something I can do to help."

"You're the master's niece," Miss Dawn insisted, but Elizabeth shook her head.

"I've never not worked a day in my life," she said. "I need to keep busy. Please, let me help."

"All right," Miss Dawn said slowly. "But there will be no dishes for you. Your hands are already hurt enough; the hot water will do nothing good for them. The master had a couple of letters that needed sending, but we ran out of stamps. If you could get some and post them, I'm sure he'd appreciate it."

"Of course," Elizabeth said. Her heart beat a little faster when she imagined going outside again, after all Joey and her uncle had said about the dangers of Birmingham over the past couple of days, but she knew that hiding inside would change nothing, and she truly did want to help. She glanced idly at the address on the front of the first letter that Miss Dawn handed to her. It was to a gentleman in London, not Birmingham, and Elizabeth felt a pang when she remembered the argument she had had with her father about her uncle and the capital, just before the attack.

The elaborate penmanship on the front of the envelope was comfortingly familiar, however. One glance at it immediately took her back to being thirteen, when she pulled the strange envelope from the hearth and learned about her uncle for the first time. Her uncle had cared so much about her that he had sent her the equivalent of more than two years' of her own father's wages, without any guarantee that it would ever actually reach her.

She was in safe hands here.

Miss Dawn fussed over her as she got ready to go out, eyeing her boots to make sure they were sturdy enough and insisting that she take a cloak in case of a sudden unseasonable chill. The sky was surprisingly grey when Elizabeth stepped outside, and she found herself thinking of Joey, stuck outside whether rain or shine. She hoped the weather held for his sake.

The post office was not far and would not take Elizabeth anywhere near where Patrick had discovered her the previous day, but she found herself looking out for Joey anyway, just in case he had chosen a different street to beg on. She saw no sign of him. Still, when she saw a small girl begging on the street, she pressed all of her change from the post office into her hand, hoping that her uncle would not object. She knew now what it was like to be cold and hungry, and the girl's delighted grin and repeated thanks made her certain that she had done the right thing.

The rest of the day was a battle of wills between her and Miss Dawn, albeit one defined by overwhelming kindness and generosity on each part. Miss Dawn wished for Elizabeth to rest and relax; Elizabeth wished to help Miss Dawn and her uncle in any way that she could. As a result, neither of them got as much done as they would have if one of them had caved to the other, but Elizabeth kept busy, and her affection for Miss Dawn grew with her every concerned comment or good-natured chastisement at Elizabeth's interference.

The whole family ate dinner in the dining room that night—Miss Dawn, too—and it did not take long before Miss Dawn was telling Uncle Arthur about Elizabeth's refusal to sit still.

"I told her that she's a guest here," Miss Dawn said, "but she will insist on tiring herself out. I don't know what to do with her."

"You mustn't exhaust yourself," Uncle Arthur said to Elizabeth with a smile. "You're a guest here. You don't need to earn your place."

"I want to be useful, Uncle," Elizabeth said.

"You're a good girl," he said. "Well, I always have errands that need running, and I'm sure Miss Dawn would appreciate some help purchasing things from the market. Fresh air is the cure for all ills, I've found, so even you could not protest to that, Miss Dawn."

"But sir—" Patrick began. Uncle Arthur laughed.

"Don't you worry, Patrick," he said. "She won't be replacing you. And there's no harm in her delivering a letter or two occasionally, now, is there?" He gave Patrick a pointed look, and Patrick blushed and looked down at his plate, nodding.

Elizabeth felt a little sorry for him, so she pushed herself to speak again. "How was your day, Uncle Arthur?" she asked.

He sighed. "Tiring, my dear," he said. "But productive. I don't know what I'd do without Patrick here to assist me, though." He smiled at Patrick, who continued to eat as though he had not heard the praise, although his ears turned slightly pinker beneath his mop of brown hair.

"What is it exactly you do?" Elizabeth asked him. "Miss Dawn told me it was something to do with the railways—"

"Oh, it's not particularly interesting," Uncle Arthur said, with a wave of his hand. "We work on engines and the like. There is quite a demand, as I'm sure you can imagine."

"I've never been on a steam train," Elizabeth said softly. "I should like to, sometime. Papa once mentioned us travelling to London, but—we never got the chance."

"Then we will take a trip," Uncle Arthur said. "Anywhere you like. London or Yorkshire or Scotland if it pleases you."

"Scotland?" Elizabeth asked.

"Of course," he said. "Wherever you like. Though work is a

little busy at the moment... perhaps in December? I've heard Edinburgh is lovely that time of year."

"I would like that very much," Elizabeth said softly.

"Then it's settled," Uncle Arthur said with a smile.

ELIZABETH FOUND it more difficult to fall asleep that night. She had slept away her exhaustion the night before, and her few errands for Miss Dawn had not been enough to tire her to her bones, leaving her to sit awake with her thoughts. She sat in a chair by the window and looked out onto the street, wondering what about the view had changed in the years since her mother had sat there. She felt closer to her mama than she had in years, dressed in her clothes, sleeping in her room, seeing the things that she must have seen before Elizabeth was born, but she felt strangely distant from memories of her father, even though he had only died a couple of days before. She was in the house of a man her father had hated, although she could not see why her father had felt that way. Perhaps it was some old bad blood, she thought. Perhaps her mother's rich older brother had been opposed to her marrying a relatively poor button merchant and it had caused a rift between them. Perhaps her brother had grown softer as he aged, and reached out after the mother's death, but, in the trauma of loss, her father had been unable to forgive him.

It was only one possibility, she thought, but it would make sense. Perhaps she should ask. But she got the feeling that discussions of her mother would be a painful, delicate subject, and she did not want to upset anyone so soon after her arrival.

She hoped that her father would forgive her for turning to her uncle in her time of need. If he had got to know Uncle Arthur as he was now, she thought, he would have liked him. And surely her father would be grateful to him for helping her, when he no longer could. Terrible things had happened over the past few days, and if Uncle Arthur had not found her, things might have been far, far worse. She had a roof over her head now, and food to eat, and company that seemed to like and value her. Her father would have appreciated that.

But thinking about her father inspired a wave of sorrow in Elizabeth that almost overwhelmed her. She squeezed her eyes closed against the tears that rushed out, and let out a long breath, searching for calm.

She had the sudden urge to stretch her legs, maybe get some more water to drink from the kitchen. She did not want Uncle Arthur to think she was snooping in his home, but, she reassured herself, she would not go anywhere she had not been shown before. The house was dark and quiet, but Elizabeth still had her candle burning, too full of thoughts to have blown it out and even attempted to sleep.

She fastened her mother's old robe over her nightgown, marvelling at the softness of the material and its rich paisley pattern. Holding her candle in her left hand, she cautiously opened her bedroom door and stepped out into the halfway.

Something moved in the shadows near the stairs, and Elizabeth let out a gasp of surprise.

"I'm sorry," Patrick's voice said, from the darkness of the stairs. "I'm so sorry, Miss Elizabeth. I didn't mean to startle you."

Her heart was racing from the shock, and she pressed her free hand to her chest, urging it to settle and slow. Patrick stepped closer, until the light from her candle illuminated his freckled face. He looked half concerned, half embarrassed by the encounter.

"Why don't you have a light?" she asked him.

"I know the house backwards," he said, "even in the dark. It seemed like a waste. I didn't think—" He swallowed. "I'm sorry to have startled you."

He was in a nightshirt, Elizabeth realised, and she found herself blushing. She looked away from him, staring instead at the way the candlelight sent shadows dancing across the wallpaper.

"No," she said, around the lump in her throat. "I'm sorry I disturbed you. This is your home. I am just—please accept my apologies." She no longer wanted to go to the kitchen. That would take her walking past Patrick, and if she got any closer, he would surely be able to hear how loudly her heart was beating. She turned back toward her room.

"Did you not want something?" Patrick asked.

"Oh, I—I was going for water," Elizabeth said. "But I just remembered, I actually have some in my room. Miss Dawn is very helpful. I should have thought before."

"Oh," Patrick said. He rubbed the back of his neck, his face red. "Well, then. Goodnight, Miss Elizabeth."

"Elizabeth," she said. "Please. It's just Elizabeth."

He nodded.

"Goodnight, Patrick," she whispered, and she hurried back into her room before he could reply.

# CHAPTER 9

*E*lizabeth soon settled into the rhythm of life at the Taylor house. Uncle Arthur and Patrick were often away at the factory, but when they were home, they spent evenings together with Elizabeth and Miss Dawn in the study, Patrick studying, Miss Dawn doing embroidery, and Uncle Arthur regaling them with tales from his youth. Elizabeth's talent with a needle was soon put to good use, and her stitches proved so quick and neat that she soon took over from Miss Dawn as the resident mender of the household. Miss Dawn joked that Elizabeth was going to put her out of a job with her superior talent, but she smiled as she said it, and Elizabeth knew that Miss Dawn was an integral part of the house, and would never be replaced, not even if she never sewed another stitch or chopped another potato in her life.

Elizabeth felt awkward around Patrick after their unexpected late-night run-in, and from the way he looked away from her and blushed whenever she entered the room, she guessed that he felt the same way too. Uncle Arthur chuckled to himself whenever he saw the pair of them look away from one another, blushing despite themselves, but he never commented.

Miss Dawn, on the other hand, started commenting to Elizabeth about how Patrick was such a nice young man at every opportunity.

Elizabeth did not need the prompting. She had spent her teenage years mildly fascinated by the freckled boy who worked for her uncle, and now that he was a more constant fixture in her life, she found herself watching him when he was not looking and admiring what she saw. He was no poet with his words, but then, neither was Elizabeth, and Elizabeth quickly saw the care and love he carried in his heart, the solidness of his nature behind his shyness.

But, she told herself firmly, it was foolish to think of her uncle's apprentice as anything other than a friend.

One evening, about six weeks after Elizabeth first arrived at her uncle's home, she walked into the study to find Patrick sitting in front of the hearth, poking a stubbornly small fire with the poker. Uncle Arthur and Miss Dawn were not there.

"Stupid thing," Patrick muttered to himself. He clearly had not heard Elizabeth enter.

"Can I help?" Elizabeth asked softly. Patrick jumped.

"Miss Elizabeth," he said. "I didn't see you there."

"That's all right," she said softly. "What's the problem with the fire?"

"It's stubborn, is what it is," Patrick muttered, almost to himself. "I'm sorry, Miss Elizabeth. I'll get out of your hair."

"No," Elizabeth said quickly. "Don't be silly. You were here first. But where are the others?"

"Your uncle is working late tonight," Patrick said, "but he said he didn't need me. And Miss Dawn has gone to lie down, I think. She said her head's feeling a little delicate. But if you want to use the study, miss, I can finish up with the fire and be on my way."

"Of course not," Elizabeth said. "Why would I want you to leave?" She felt herself blushing slightly and strode over to the fireplace to try and cover her sudden embarrassment. She considered the arrangement of logs there and smiled. "Don't you know how to build a good hearth, Mr. Patrick?" she asked. "Here." She used the poker to nudge the logs into a more hospitable position and smiled wider as the flame caught. Soon, the room would be flooded with warmth.

"You don't have to call me Mr. Patrick," Patrick said. "Unless you want to, that is. You're the master's niece, after all. But I would like it if you just called me Patrick."

"That's strange," Elizabeth said, "because I'm sure I recall telling you to just call me Elizabeth, and yet you call me *miss*. I was just following your example."

Patrick's face burned, and Elizabeth gently touched his elbow and smiled to make sure he knew that she was joking. "Elizabeth is fine, Patrick."

He nodded, and then stood up abruptly. "I should do my reading," he said.

Elizabeth nodded, feeling a little disappointed, although she could not have said why. She collected some of her own sewing from the basket beside her usual armchair and settled in, tucking her legs onto the seat under her skirt as she began to sew. For a while, they sat in companionable silence, accompanied by the light crackle of the fire.

"You know, Patrick," she said slowly, her eyes still fixed on her work. "I hardly know anything about you. I don't even know your full name."

"Smith," he said. "Patrick Smith. Not a very exciting name."

"As a Green whose mother was a Taylor," Elizabeth said, "I can hardly comment on having a common surname."

"But Green suits you," he said earnestly. "It sounds—it sounds like you. Pretty. I mean—" Elizabeth looked up in time to see Patrick look away, back at his books, looking mortified. "It's a pretty name."

"Thank you," Elizabeth said softly. They worked in a silence for another few minutes, and then Elizabeth dared to break it again. "What about your family, Patrick?" she asked. "How—how did you end up here with my uncle?" Patrick did not answer for a moment, and Elizabeth had a sudden fear that her question had been too personal or too painful. He did not have to share details of his life with her, if he did not choose to. "I'm sorry," she said quickly. "I shouldn't pry."

"No," Patrick said. "It's all right. But I never really had a family, that I can remember. I must've become an orphan when I was very small. Grew up in the orphanage for a few years, and then the master came by, looking for a young apprentice, and I don't know why, but for some reason he chose me and offered me the job."

"Probably because you're smart," Elizabeth said. "And capable, and hardworking. He must have seen that."

Patrick bit his lip, looking stubbornly at his book. "Well, I don't know about that," he said. "But I'm grateful to him."

Elizabeth placed her sewing on the arm of the chair and stood. Patrick looked up at her in surprise as she slowly crossed the room toward him. "What are you studying?" she asked.

"Oh, it's um—" He held up the book, and Elizabeth slowly read the writing on the cover: *The Rise and Fall of the Roman Empire, Vol. 1*. "It's about the Romans. You know, the—the ancient people who lived in Italy two thousand years ago."

She smiled. "I thought you were learning about being Uncle Arthur's apprentice."

"Sometimes I am," Patrick said quickly. "Well, I still am now, I suppose, in a way. He thinks an apprentice and a businessman should both understand things like history too. He says it gives them a better chance of understanding the world. And I just—I find it interesting."

"I don't know anything about that," Elizabeth said, a little sadly. "I never went to school. My mama taught me how to read and write, but I didn't have much to practice with. I can do sums and things, from working in the button shop."

"You know other things," Patrick said. "Far more useful things than stuffy old books about people who are long dead. But I could lend you the book after I'm done," he said. "If you would like."

Elizabeth looked at the thickness of the spine and the tiny print she could not see over Patrick's shoulder, and she shook her head. "I don't think I would do very well with it," she said. "But—" she hesitated. "*You* can tell me about it when you're done. If you like."

Patrick's ears turned pink, but he nodded. "All right," he said.

# CHAPTER 10

*A*fter their conversation in the study, Elizabeth and Patrick began to talk more often. On evenings when Uncle Arthur was away with work, she and Patrick would sit in armchairs next to one another in the study, discussing whatever he was reading while Elizabeth sewed and Miss Dawn kept an eye on them from the other side of the room with a soft smile on her face. Sometimes, Patrick would read particularly interesting passages out loud to her, and although Elizabeth sometimes thought that the author of these books must have actually, secretly disliked the Romans to have written something so dry, Patrick's enthusiasm brought it to life. He looked at Elizabeth every few seconds as he read, his cheeks flushed, as though checking her enjoyment, and Elizabeth's own cheeks flushed with pleasure at the attention. They still could not speak to one another entirely smoothly, but Patrick had stopped calling her *Miss Elizabeth*, at least, and Elizabeth felt a rush of warmth in her chest every time he glanced at her. She found that she liked the slightly stumbling awkwardness between them. It made Patrick all the more endearing, and his attention even more worth pursuing.

Outside of the family evenings together, Elizabeth tried to keep herself as busy as possible. The loss of her father clung to her like a shadow. Being still allowed Elizabeth time to remember him and feel his loss, and when she remembered him, she wondered that she did not collapse to her knees from the rush and weight of the pain that struck her. One day, Uncle Arthur promised her, she would be able to think of her father with fondness and warmth, not pain, as he was now able to think of Elizabeth's mother after initially being torn apart by her loss. But time, he told her, was the only path to such peace.

But although thoughts of her father caused her great pain, Elizabeth found herself feeling closer to her mother than she had in years. Her Uncle Arthur had her mother's eyes, but she also recognised other traits of her mother in him, things she had almost forgotten in the years since her sudden death. He had her mother's kindness and generosity, and sometimes, when he spoke or laughed, Elizabeth heard a tone in him that sent her flying back in her mind to being six years old and seeing her mother's delight.

Three months after Elizabeth first arrived at Uncle Arthur's, Patrick returned from work early. When Elizabeth heard the front door opening, she hurried down the stairs to the front hallway, curious at who had arrived, and then stopped halfway down the stairs, startled, when she saw Patrick's appearance.

He was not wearing a jacket, and his shirtsleeve was torn almost from elbow to wrist. She thought he looked a little paler than usual, too, as though he were in shock.

"Patrick!" she cried, as she ran the rest of the way to the hall. "What happened?"

Patrick grimaced. "I was just clumsy," he said. "Not paying attention to what I was doing. My sleeve caught on a machine at the factory."

"Are you hurt?" Elizabeth asked. She hurried forward and gently took hold of his arm to inspect the skin through the tear.

It looked thankfully undamaged, without a single bruise or speck of blood, but Elizabeth continued holding onto it and staring, as though the true extent of the damage might reveal itself if she looked carefully enough.

"No," Patrick said, a little hoarsely. "I'm all right. It only caught my sleeve."

"How could you be so foolish?" Elizabeth cried. "It could have taken your whole arm off." She did not know precisely what machines they used at her uncle's factory, but she had heard enough horror stories of workers who got their clothes caught in the mechanisms and lost limbs or worse as a result.

"I'm sorry," Patrick said softly. "I'm all right."

Elizabeth suddenly realised that she was still holding onto his arm. She released it quickly, before he thought she was being too forward. If he did not think that already. "But you might not have been," she said, in a slightly quieter, calmer voice. "You shouldn't take risks."

Patrick nodded. and Elizabeth felt suddenly self-conscious. He might not appreciate her chastising him. But really, he *should* be more careful. Terrible things could happen to someone at a factory if they did not have their wits about them, and she absolutely did not want to lose him.

"Hand it over to me," Elizabeth said, "and I'll mend it for you now." Patrick stared at her, his face suddenly red, and Elizabeth blushed too as she realised the implications of what she had said. "I mean—please, go upstairs and get changed, and bring me your shirt back so I can fix it." She wasn't sure that attempt had been better. He was still blushing, and now she was imagining Patrick pulling his shirt off over his head, revealing whatever muscles lay beneath.

But Patrick did not argue. He nodded, and she stepped aside to allow him to stride up the stairs. Elizabeth paced the hallway in his absence, torn between horror at what might have happened to him, and horror at what she had said. Patrick emerged about five minutes later, holding the torn shirt in his hands, and mercifully dressed in both a new shirt and a waistcoat. He handed the shirt to Elizabeth, and then followed her to the study, where she sat and began her work.

"You can mend it, can't you?" Patrick said. "It's a bad tear."

"I can mend it," Elizabeth said, "but I'm going to put one stitch out of place, just for you. That way when you look at your shirtsleeve, you'll remember what happened and be reminded to be careful. We can't fix your arm as easily as this."

Elizabeth worked quickly, and Patrick fell into a comfortable silence beside her. Elizabeth thought perhaps she was a little too aware of his presence, though, especially the way his arm was draped on the side of her own chair, mere inches from her elbow.

"There," she said, once she was done. "Almost as good as new. But don't make me do it again."

"I won't, Miss Elizabeth," Patrick said. "I promise." She scowled at being called *miss* again, and he laughed. He turned to walk back upstairs, and then he paused. "Um, actually," he said, without looking back. "I was wondering. Since I'm finished with work for the day, and it's a nice day outside—the leaves are changing on the trees, you know, and it's fairly warm for October—maybe you would like to go for a walk?"

"A walk?" Elizabeth repeated.

He nodded. "There are some small gardens nearby that we can go to. I think you'd like them."

"All right," Elizabeth said. "Yes. That would be lovely."

Patrick looked surprised by her easy agreement, and then he smiled widely. "All right then," he said. "Let me just—put this away then, and maybe we can go?"

"I'll get my boots," Elizabeth said with a smile.

# CHAPTER 11

*P*atrick held out his arm to Elizabeth as they stepped out onto the street, and she took it, feeling a little thrill in her chest as she did so. Patrick's arm was warm beneath his sleeve, and she could not help feeling a little bit like a fancy lady as she strode down the street with a man to accompany her.

Patrick led her a few streets away, then stopped outside a curve-topped, solid iron gate, halfway along a brick wall that was too tall for Elizabeth to see over. "Are you certain we're allowed in here?" she asked, as Patrick pushed open the gate, and then reached around the inside to release the chain that held it ajar.

"These gardens belong to a friend of your uncle's," he said, as he released the catch on the chain and opened the gate fully. "He lets us walk in them whenever we like."

Elizabeth followed him through the gate, and then stopped, taking in the sight before her. The garden contained several oak trees, their leaves a riot of red and orange, the ground beneath them scattered with acorns, and the path lined with rosebushes. The other plant beds contained beautiful purple flowers that she thought might have been irises, and chrysanthemums in pink and yellow and white. The path meandering between the various trees and flowerbeds were lined with loose pebbles, and she could see a bench against one wall, under the shade of an oak tree, with a small fountain filled with fish directly before it.

"This is beautiful," Elizabeth said. "I've never seen so much nature in all my life."

Patrick grinned. "I thought you might like it. Some people think there aren't many flowers in October, but they just don't know the right ones to look for." He held out his arm for Elizabeth again, and she took it as they began to stroll deeper into the garden.

Elizabeth was captivated by the beauty of the flowers around her, and she paused frequently to gently touch the soft petals or to savour the scent coming from the blooms. She picked a few acorns off the ground and tucked them into her pocket to keep, and once the clatter of the gate opening and closing had faded, she began to hear birdsong, and see the odd flash of feathers in the trees.

"It's magical," Elizabeth sighed. Patrick led her over to the bench by the fountain, but they did not sit. She was too captivated by the splashing of the water. A few fallen oak leaves floated on the surface, and the remaining canopy above them cast dappled shadow and light over the fountain and the ground. "What does Uncle Arthur do that other people don't, to have such rich and generous friends?"

She did not intend it as a serious question, speaking the words lightly, almost carelessly, but she paused when she glanced up at Patrick's face and saw that he had paled slightly, the freedom and joy in his expression gone.

"I suppose being rich brings you rich friends," Elizabeth added, in a slightly less certain voice. "Though I'm certain many people would like to know the secret to that too."

Patrick laughed, but it sounded a little forced. "Yes," he said.

"I'd—I'd like to know that too. Buy a whole garden like this just for myself." He still seemed flustered, and after a long pause, he strode away. "Let me show you my favourite flower in the whole garden," he said. "I think you'll like it."

Elizabeth followed him, a little hesitantly, as he led her to a patch of tall, soft-blue irises. The edges of each petal were a gentle blue, their centres white, the colours fading from one to the other. "This one," Patrick said. "I've always liked it, but—it's my favourite now. The colour... it's exactly like the colour of your eyes."

"Which part?" Elizabeth joked, even as her heart began to flutter at the affection in his words. Patrick reached out and touched a spot near the edge of a petal, brushing a pale crystal blue.

"Just here," he said. Elizabeth turned to look at his face, and she realised that they were standing close together, their arms almost touching. She looked up into his eyes, and he looked back at her, smiling softly. "Yes," he said. "The colour is exactly right."

Elizabeth felt a fluttering in her chest. She did not step away. Patrick's gaze flicked down to look at her lips, and she felt a thrill as she realised he must be thinking of kissing her. His hand came up to gently cup her cheek, and Elizabeth felt a smile spreading across her face as he leaned slightly closer. Her heart raced with anticipation.

But then she remembered his reaction to her idle question, the way he'd changed the subject so quickly and so flatteringly. He was hiding something from her. She could not kiss a boy who could not be honest with her. She shook her head and stepped back.

"I'm sorry," Patrick said. "I didn't mean to be so forward—"

"No," Elizabeth said. "No, it's all right. But maybe—perhaps we should return home."

Patrick nodded, not looking at her.

They walked home side by side, but he did not offer her his arm again.

ELIZABETH DID NOT MENTION the incident to Miss Dawn or Uncle Arthur, but it lingered in her thoughts. Patrick was hiding something, some terrible details about her uncle's friend and his wealth. She thought again of the vagueness of his description of his work, and the way her father had insisted she never meet him. It left her with a slight uncertain chill that made it difficult for her to settle.

And then Patrick had almost kissed her. That thought was thrilling and terrifying too. Did he have real feelings for her, or had he just been trying to distract her from questions about her uncle? She could not believe that Patrick would do such a thing, and he did seem to genuinely enjoy her company. But how could she trust him, when she knew he was hiding something from her?

She and Patrick did not speak beyond polite, awkward greetings for several days, until one evening Elizabeth stepped into the study to find Patrick reading alone.

"Oh," she mumbled. "I'm sorry," and she began to back out of the room, until Patrick stood up.

"Please, wait," he said. "I'm the one's who's sorry. I never meant to make you uncomfortable. I made assumptions, and—"

"No," Elizabeth said, shaking her head. "No, it isn't like that. You didn't make any false assumptions." She hesitated in the doorway. "But—you changed the subject so quickly. I knew you were hiding something from me."

Patrick looked down at the ground, his shoulders slumping. "I'm sorry," he said.

"I was afraid," Elizabeth said, "that perhaps you—perhaps you were just trying to distract me with your words."

"No," Patrick said. "That isn't true."

She nodded, not quite looking at him. "Then can you tell me?" she said. "What was it that upset you?"

Patrick did not speak for a long moment, and when Elizabeth looked up, she saw he was looking at the fireplace, smiling sadly. "I wish I could tell you," he said. "But I cannot."

"Why not?" she asked.

He shook his head slowly. "I cannot tell you that either. But one day—one day I hope it won't matter any more. And when that happens, I would like to tell you."

"Is it something dangerous?" Elizabeth asked softly.

Patrick did not reply for a long moment, and her stomach sank. Then he said: "What do you want, Elizabeth, for the future? I'm certain you're always welcome to remain with us, but—what would you like?"

"I always wanted to go to London," she said. "See somewhere new."

"I think that sounds like a wonderful idea," Patrick said, and Elizabeth felt her heart sink further as she realised he wanted her to move away. Had he been lying to her, about how he cared? Or was the truth so terrible that he would rather she leave than have to tell her?

Where exactly did her uncle's wealth come from? What was so dangerous that she could not know?

She nodded at him, no longer willing to press the point. If he did not want to tell her, he would not. "All right," she said. "Maybe I will. Have a good evening, Patrick."

She turned and was almost out of the door when she heard his soft reply. "You too, Miss Elizabeth," he said.

# CHAPTER 12

*E*lizabeth tried to forget their conversation and act as normally as possible around her uncle and the rest of the household, but she became increasingly tense every time Uncle Arthur stayed out late for work or spoke vaguely over what *exactly* it was that he did. She found herself lying awake at night, worrying about Patrick and her uncle and what exactly he had done in the past to make her father hate him so much.

One evening, a few weeks after her conversation with Patrick, Elizabeth found herself alone in the study with her uncle. Patrick had come down with a bad head cold, and Miss Dawn had retired early with her new Indian rubber hot water bottle to aid the pain in her back, so Uncle Arthur and Elizabeth spent the dying moments of the day by the fire together, him reading, her working on a new dress for herself.

As the clock ticked toward ten, Uncle Arthur looked up from his book and watched Elizabeth working for a long moment, a gentle smile spreading across his face. It took a little while for Elizabeth to notice that he was watching her, absorbed in her sewing as she was. When she looked up at her uncle, his smile grew.

"You are so much like your mother," he said softly. "She was always so talented too, and so kind and peaceful. Just like you."

Elizabeth found herself smiling back. "Thank you," she said. "I always hope I might make her proud."

"She would be beyond proud of you," her uncle said. "She would have treasured you. She did treasure you, every moment she could." He looked away, into the flames of the fire. "I adored your mother. She was one of the best people I ever knew. Although she was a nightmare of a little sibling at times."

"Really?" Elizabeth asked. She could not imagine her mother ever causing any trouble.

"Oh, yes," Uncle Arthur said, with a chuckle. "She was always jealous that I would get to go out to business meetings with your grandfather while she had to remain at home—she was about four at the time, mind—so she took to hiding my shoes from me so I couldn't leave without her. I ended up having to squirrel away my own shoes somewhere secret so that she couldn't hide them from me, and then she'd get so angry and stomp all around the house looking for them."

"I can't imagine it," Elizabeth said, smiling.

"She was a nightmare with sweets as well. She would always offer me a pear drop from her paper bag from the shop, and then run away as soon as I tried to take it."

"Didn't you eventually learn that it was a trick?"

"I did," Uncle Arthur said. "But I was a ten-year-old boy. I was always hungry for sweets. I couldn't risk the possibility that she really was offering me one this time and I'd end up missing out. Besides," he added, his smile growing even warmer. "It would ruin the fun of her game, wouldn't it? She had me wrapped around her little finger, even then." He shook his head fondly.

"What happened, Uncle Arthur?" Elizabeth asked tentatively. "Why did I never meet you before she died?"

"You did meet me," he said, "when you were very small. Too

small to remember, I'm sure. You were a beautiful baby. But your mother—she wanted to take her own path in life. We had a disagreement, and—" He swallowed hard. Tears were forming in his eyes. "I'll always regret those years we lost before her death."

"But why?" Elizabeth whispered. "What happened between you? Why did my father hate you so much?"

Uncle Arthur gave her a sad smile. "I made a mistake," he said. "But what does it matter anymore? It is too late to mend the past now. All I can do is try my best to make amends in the here and now."

Elizabeth considered him quietly for a moment. It was not the answer she had been hoping for. The need to know *why* still burned within her, fuelled by Patrick's strange behaviour and the mystery over how, exactly, Uncle Arthur had become so rich. But Uncle Arthur was standing, placing his book safely down on the table beside his armchair. "It's getting late, Elizabeth," he said. "We should both be getting our rest."

Elizabeth knew a dismissal when she heard one. She nodded and stood, too, but even as she bid him goodnight, she desperately wished he would tell her the truth.

She retired to bed, and a few minutes later, she heard the sound of Uncle Arthur's footsteps heading to his own room to rest. But Elizabeth could not sleep. She could not stop running through that conversation with Uncle Arthur in her mind, smiling at his memories of her mother, and worrying over what could have been so terrible that it had torn a rift between the siblings that had never healed.

After the clock chimed midnight, Elizabeth heard footsteps in the hallway outside her room again. At first, she thought nothing of them. Anyone might be wandering the house for any number of reasons, and if Miss Dawn or Patrick were heading down to the kitchen to get hot milk to help them to sleep, she might well join them. Then, a minute later, she heard the front door of the house swing open and then click shut. The sound was quiet enough that Elizabeth probably would not have even noticed it if she had not already been listening, as though whoever opened it did so carefully, trying not to be heard.

Elizabeth hurried to her bedroom window and peered through the gap in the curtains. The streetlamps outside illuminated the pavement. Her uncle was striding down the street, fully dressed, his gait determined.

Where could her uncle possibly be heading after midnight?

Elizabeth sank into the armchair in her room, her legs shaking. Ice-cold fear flooded her chest. A secret journey outside the house in the middle of the night... it could not be *good*, could it?

But, she tried to tell herself, she was probably jumping to conclusions. There were many reasons a gentleman might leave the house in the middle of the night. Not all of them were proper, and she did not necessarily want to contemplate them in too much detail, but it was not necessarily something *dangerous*.

She sat up by the window, knowing she would not be able to sleep a wink until her uncle returned, and waited. A couple of hours later, she heard footsteps on the street outside, and she looked out just in time to see her uncle opening the front door. She listened as he moved around downstairs for a short while, before heading up again.

Elizabeth held her breath as she heard him pass her room, as though he might somehow sense that she was awake and listening. But he walked past without pause, leaving Elizabeth to sit and wonder just what precisely was going on.

∼

"You're quieter than usual this morning," Miss Dawn commented to her as the pair ate breakfast the following day. Despite his late-night outing, Uncle Arthur had already departed the house by the time Elizabeth awoke, taking Patrick with him. She had to admit that she was relieved. She did not know how she would react when she finally saw him. Miss Dawn's sympathy was much easier to handle.

"I'm just tired," Elizabeth said, forcing herself to smile slightly. "I didn't sleep well."

"I hope you aren't coming down with anything, dear," Miss Dawn said. She hurried forward and pressed the back of her hand to Elizabeth's forehead. "You don't feel too warm, at least."

"I'm all right," Elizabeth said. "Sometimes I simply get too caught up in my own thoughts to sleep, that's all."

"Oh, I know how you feel," Miss Dawn said, nodding sagely. "I used to be such a worrywart when I was your age. Always fretting about something, almost making myself sick with the *what ifs*. But one good thing about getting older is that it gives you a little more perspective. Sitting up and worrying about things has never changed a single thing in my life, except to make me tired out from my fretting. My advice, Miss Elizabeth, is think about what you can actually *do* to sort out your worries. And if it's nothing, well, then the world will play out in its own way whether you worry or not, so you might as well save yourself the pain. Now eat up that porridge. Some good warm food can only help."

ELIZABETH THOUGHT over Miss Dawn's words over the next few days. What could she actually do about Uncle Arthur's strange behaviour? She could ask him about it, but she did not entirely trust him to tell the truth, and Patrick had already shown he would not betray his master's secrets for her sake. She took to sitting up late, listening to see if her uncle headed out again, and was horrified several days later when she heard not one but two sets of footsteps walking down the hall late one night. She hurried to the window and peered out between the curtains in time to see Uncle Arthur depart the house with Patrick at his side.

She would have liked to believe that Uncle Arthur would not be doing anything dangerous if Patrick was with him, but it did not quite feel like truth. She remembered the tear in Patrick's shirt, the cloth near ruined but his skin perfectly unharmed, and her stomach sank as she wondered if that had been a lie too. Not a factory accident, perhaps, but something more sinister.

She heard Uncle Arthur leave late at night several more times over the following few weeks. Sometimes, he was accompanied by Patrick. Usually, he was alone. Uncle Arthur noticed that Elizabeth had become quieter than usual during their evening gatherings in the study, but she responded to his concern with a few words about missing her father, and he did not press her again.

And still, Elizabeth contemplated Miss Dawn's advice. There had to be *something* she could do.

She could follow him, she realised. That would answer all of her questions about his destination. The idea seemed reckless, too bold, but Miss Dawn had been right. She could not simply sit and fret. She needed to act, or she needed to forget what she knew, and she knew she would not be able to forget.

The first night that Elizabeth sat up late, still dressed and ready to run out of the door at a moment's notice, her uncle did not stir. But the second night, around midnight, she heard the tell-tale sound of footsteps in the hallway. She closed her eyes and listened, hoping, *praying* that it was only Uncle Arthur, and that Patrick was not with him. She could only hear one set of feet.

She waited until the front door opened and closed and peered out of the window to check her uncle's direction before sneaking out of her room and down the stairs. She pulled her boots on with frantic haste, threw a cloak over her shoulders, and slipped out of the door.

By this time, Uncle Arthur was almost at the end of the street. Elizabeth crept behind him, not wanting to get close enough for him to see her, terrified that if she stayed back, she would lose him. She sent out her thanks to all the scientists of the British Empire, as the gas lamps perfectly illuminated the way, allowing her to see her uncle even at a distance, but still providing shadows for her to walk in.

It was late November, and the night air was frigidly cold. Elizabeth could see her breath clouding in front of her face, and she wrapped her cloak tightly around herself. Her uncle was walking rather briskly, and she found herself running at points to keep up with him. Her heart raced, but even she could not have said whether she was more afraid of being discovered, or of what she might discover when they reached her uncle's destination.

She followed him through winding streets toward the heart of the city. Then her uncle stopped abruptly and turned to look at the road behind him—the road where Elizabeth now stood. Elizabeth darted into the shadows and pressed herself flat against the wall, but she felt certain that she had been too slow. He must have seen her. Why else would he have looked back at all? She held her breath, praying for him to turn around, to continue on his way without noticing her, and after a moment, he turned and made his way around the corner, into another side alley.

Elizabeth hurried after him again, unable to believe her luck. But when she reached this last turning, she stopped suddenly. This alley was a dead end, illuminated only by the moon and the stars, and Uncle Arthur was not alone. He stood a few feet away from another man. It was too dark to see him clearly, but Elizabeth felt certain she had never met him before. The moonlight illuminated his face just enough for her to see a large scar across it, from above his right eye down to his mouth, and Elizabeth knew this was not a face she would easily forget.

She could not hear what her uncle and this man were saying, but both of them looked tense. Her uncle reached into his pocket and pulled something out—money, she thought, a pile of notes, although it was hard to be certain in the dark—and the other man took them with a nod before passing something back to him in return.

Elizabeth pressed herself against the wall at the entrance to the alley, straining her ears to pick up anything they might be saying. But they were speaking in low voices, and all she heard was a deep murmur, none of the words clear.

The man with a scar across his face looked up suddenly, glancing at the entrance to the alley where Elizabeth stood. She darted back, pressing herself flat against the wall, and held her breath. A moment later, the murmuring continued.

But Elizabeth knew she had already pressed her luck too far. She did not think her uncle would hurt her, but she could not be so certain about the stranger. If he found her eavesdropping....

And what ineffective eavesdropping it had proved anyway. She could not hear a word. But she had seen enough to guess at the nature of their meeting. They were carrying out a deal, and based on the location and the way they spoke in such low voices, she had no doubt that their activities must be criminal in nature.

Hands shaking, Elizabeth backed slowly away. As soon as she dared, without risking them hearing her footsteps, she turned and ran all the way back to her uncle's house.

# CHAPTER 13

$\mathcal{E}$lizabeth rose the following morning after barely a wink of sleep. She had been up all night, pacing her room, trying to figure out what to do. Should she confront her uncle? It seemed like the moral choice, instead of sneaking around in the dark, but how would he respond? She still had no money of her own, except for the few coins that she had earned with Joey. What would happen to her when the truth came out? Would she have to run out onto the street again?

Her arms and legs felt heavy as she descended the stairs for breakfast, and she dreaded seeing her uncle, but it seemed he had already left for his morning's business. Elizabeth's stomach twisted as she imagined precisely what that business might be.

But Patrick was still home. He smiled at her as she entered the kitchen, and if he noticed the uncertainty in her smile back at him, he did not comment on it.

"Good morning, Elizabeth," he said. "How did you sleep?"

She stared at him, unable to speak. Did he know what she had done? Patrick frowned at her hesitation, looking suddenly concerned, and she forced herself to speak. "Well enough," she said. "You?"

"I slept well enough too," he said, with a guileless smile.

"Neither of you young things get enough sleep, if you ask me," Miss Dawn said from where she stood near the hearth. "You all stress and fret far too much." She pushed a bowl of porridge into Elizabeth's hands. "Sit," she said. "Eat. You look dead on your feet, and it's only eight in the morning."

Elizabeth sat at the table in the kitchen, too tired and hungry to argue, while Patrick smiled fondly at the older woman. "Thanks so much for the food, Miss Dawn," he said. "It really helped."

"Oh, go on with you and your sweet talk," Miss Dawn said with faux sternness.

"I do have work to do," Patrick agreed. He turned and smiled at Elizabeth, gave her a slightly uncertain little bow, and left the room.

Elizabeth ate her breakfast, mostly without speaking. Miss Dawn chattered away to her, but she only seemed to require the minimal number of *I sees* and *really?s* from Elizabeth, and Elizabeth was happy to provide them. Once the porridge was gone, Miss Dawn smiled at her again, and asked if she would mind going into town to fetch some fresh bread from the bakery.

"I've got a hankering for that delicious loaf they sell at Mr. Campbell's—you know the one, not far from St. Mary's? It will go so well with supper tonight. I would walk there myself, but my old joints are aching something fierce this morning. You young things don't know how lucky you are. And besides, you look as though the fresh air would do you good."

"Of course, Miss Dawn," Elizabeth said with a tired smiled. "I would be happy to go."

The deep chill of the previous night had eased with the rising of the sun, but it was still cold enough that Elizabeth was grateful for her gloves, and soon pulled the hood of her cloak up to warm her ears. Plenty of people were out and about, and Elizabeth found herself glancing at the faces of each person she passed, as though she might see that unforgettable scar.

There was a small queue at the bakery, but Elizabeth eventually emerged with two steaming hot loaves to warm her on the journey home, and a clearer head after a healthy dose of fresh air and the enticing aroma of baking bread. As she turned to head for home, she glanced up and saw Joey sitting across the street, begging for coins.

Elizabeth had not seen Joey once in the months since she had spent those nights on the streets, although she looked for him every time she came into town. It had worried her a little, although she had tried to reassure herself that he was absent for *good* reasons, not for bad ones, so it was both relieving and a little heart breaking to see him sitting there unchanged.

"Hello, Joey," she said to him as she walked over.

He looked up and grinned at her, revealing his broken teeth. "Look who it is. Doing well for yourself, I see. Tha's good. Streets are no place for a kind-hearted girl like you."

"I've been looking for you," Elizabeth said.

Joey shrugged. "I move about a lot," he said. "Can't have the police seeing you too often, or they get bored and actually decide to implement those vagrancy laws."

Elizabeth reached into her pocket and pulled out several coins to drop in his hat. Joey grinned at her. "Thank you kindly, miss." Then he frowned, his expression suddenly far more serious. "How are you getting along with Mr. Taylor?"

"Well enough," Elizabeth said, with only a little hesitancy in her voice. "He and his apprentice are kind." Then she paused and frowned. "How do you know his name?"

Joey gave a bark of laughter. "He mentioned it, girl, when he ran off with you before. I never forget a name or a face. Never know when it might be useful!"

Elizabeth could not remember that first interaction with Uncle Arthur particularly clearly, so she could not have said that

Joey's words were untrue, but there was something guarded in his expression, something forced in his laughter, that made her suspect he was not telling her the whole story.

"Do you know my uncle?" she asked.

"No, miss," Joey replied. "Can't say that I've had that pleasure."

But Elizabeth remembered Joey's expression when she had first left with Uncle Arthur. He had seemed almost nervous. But, of course, she could not prove it, and if she argued, she felt certain he would deny it even more.

She glanced around, reaching for something else to say, and her eyes fell on a nearby wall, covered with bills and graffiti. There, in the middle of the wall, was the scarred man's face.

She hurried over to it, ignoring Joey's cry of confusion. It was a wanted poster. The bill did not say what the man was wanted for, but beneath the sketch of his face, it said that he was incredibly dangerous, and that anyone with any information should inform the police at once. His name was simply listed as "Jack."

Elizabeth's whole body shook as she stared at it. Here was her proof. Her undeniable proof that her uncle was involved with criminals, *dangerous* ones. She reached forward and tore the paper off the wall, then strode back over to Joey, brandishing the picture at him.

"Do you know this man?" she asked him. "This Jack?"

A shadow seemed to fall over Joey's face as he looked at the poster. "If I'd known that was there," he said, "I wouldn't have sat 'ere, not at all."

"Who is he?"

"Jack?" Joey chuckled darkly. "He was one of the men who showed up and burned my shop. I could never forget that face."

Elizabeth felt sick. "And my uncle?" she asked. "How do you know him?"

"His face is a bit less memorable, girl," Joey said. "But I know what you're asking. He was there that night too."

Elizabeth swayed on her feet. Joey had told her that his carpenter's shop had been burned to the ground by a criminal gang. A random attack, he said. An attack painfully similar to the one that had taken her father.

Was Uncle Arthur connected with them both?

"Thank you," she said faintly. "Thank you for telling me." She dropped the warm loaves at his side. "Please, take these. I find— I have no appetite anymore. Excuse me."

"Now don't go doing anything foolish, girl," he said. "This ain't something you want to get yourself involved with."

"I'm already involved with it," Elizabeth said. She shook her head, struggling to think. "I—thank you, Joey. Again. I hope I'll see you again soon."

And with Joey shouting after her, she turned and ran for home, the wanted poster still clutched in her hand.

# CHAPTER 14

The run back to Uncle Arthur's house passed in a blur, and soon she found herself standing on the doorstep, fighting to catch her breath. She strode inside, and was half pleased, half terrified when she saw Uncle Arthur's cloak hanging from the coat stand. In her absence, he had returned home.

"Uncle Arthur?" she shouted.

"In here, Elizabeth," he said from the study.

She strode across the hallway, steeling her resolve. Uncle Arthur was working at a desk inside, writing some correspondence, but he paused and smiled at her when she entered. That smile froze on his face when he saw the fury in her expression.

"Whatever's the matter, Elizabeth?" he asked her.

His innocent concern only incensed her more. She marched over to him and slammed the wanted poster down onto the desk beside him. "Why did you meet with this man last night?"

Her uncle gaped at her. "Elizabeth, what—"

"Don't try to lie to me," she said. "I know you go out and meet criminals in the night. I followed you. I saw him."

"You followed me?" Uncle Arthur said. "Elizabeth, it isn't safe! You could have been hurt."

"And whose fault would that have been?" Elizabeth said. "You were the one meeting this man in a dark alley."

Uncle Arthur frowned. "I did leave in the night to meet a man," he said. "He needed help, and—"

"I said don't lie to me," Elizabeth said. "Please, Uncle. I *saw* you. I saw him. His face is unmistakable."

Uncle Arthur sighed. "You're right," Uncle Arthur said. "I am sorry, Elizabeth. I never wanted you to be in any danger."

"But I was!" she said. "I spoke to Joey. Do you remember him? The man who saved me when I was on the street? He used to have a good life, until some criminal thugs burned everything he owned to the ground. And do you know what he told me? He said this man—" she jabbed her finger at the image – "was the one responsible. Do you know what else he told me? He told me that you were there too. You destroyed that man's life!"

Uncle Arthur put his face into his hands. "I have destroyed many lives, Elizabeth," he said. "I am not proud of it. But that is why you cannot put yourself at risk like this. It is too dangerous for you to know all of these things. Someone might hurt you! Too many people have been hurt. I cannot risk losing you too."

Elizabeth shook her head, fighting back furious tears. "It isn't fair to me, Uncle Arthur. I need to know the truth. How could you have hurt Joey, Uncle? That man saved my life."

"I did not want to," Uncle Arthur said heavily. "I did not mean to. But things have been out of my control for too long now."

"You destroyed his life," Elizabeth said again. "Who else have you hurt?" She hesitated. "Me? My father?"

Uncle Arthur did not reply, and Elizabeth's stomach sank.

"Why did those men attack us?" she asked, in a low, steady voice.

"Please, Elizabeth," he said. "There are some things that we are better off not knowing."

"Please," she said. "Tell me."

"They were—a rival gang," Uncle Arthur said. "They wanted revenge on me, and they must have learned that you were my niece. They targeted you to hurt me."

Tears burned in Elizabeth's eyes. "That's why my father insisted we have nothing to do with you," she said. "He wanted to make sure that never happened. And it happened anyway."

"I am so sorry, Elizabeth," he said. "I know I can never make amends for what I've done. I've tried to get out of this criminal world before, but there is no way out. Once a man tries to leave, he's lucky if his associates only hurt *him*. More likely, they go after the people you care about instead. I could not risk it. Not after—not after last time."

"Last time?" Elizabeth asked. "What do you mean, last time?" Uncle Arthur did not immediately reply, and Elizabeth had a sudden thought that left her feeling like a bucket of ice-cold water had been dropped over her. "Mama," she said softly. "What happened to mama. It wasn't random, was it? It was you."

Uncle Arthur nodded, and the world around Elizabeth seemed to sway. She reached out and grabbed the top of the desk to hold herself steady as she stared at her uncle.

"I wanted to get out," he said. "I tried my best. But they knew that Lily was my sister, and that I loved her more than anything. Your mother did not approve of where my money came from, when she learned about it. I rarely saw her, but she would come to me occasionally, begging me to reconsider. She finally convinced me, but an associate must have seen her, and before I knew it—well. Not only did we lose her, but the police wouldn't even investigate. They knew the gangs were involved. There are not words to express how sorry I am, Elizabeth."

"Apologies won't bring her back," she said. "They won't bring either of them back."

Uncle Arthur nodded. "I know," he said. "After what happened, I wanted to do anything I could to support you, but your father, understandably, did not want my help. When I heard about the attack on the shop—"

Elizabeth flinched as though he had struck her. "You *knew* about it?"

"Not before it happened," he said. "But I learned of it afterward. I learned that you had escaped. I was determined to find you, to take care of you however I could. It would not undo what I had caused, but it was the least I could do."

"You are right," Elizabeth said. "It was the least you could do. If you truly cared, you would not have let my mother be murdered in vain, only for my father to be murdered several years later for almost the precise same reason." She hesitated again. She felt sick to her stomach, but there were still more questions she needed to ask, no matter how much she might fear the answers. "What happened to my father?" she asked. "Do you know? I never found him."

"I do not know exactly," Uncle Arthur said. "I only know they would not have moved him if he had survived. They would have left him in the building to burn. I am sorry, Elizabeth."

Elizabeth fought back a sob. She had known her father was dead for several months now, but with no body, no actual *proof*, a tiny part of her heart had always held out hope that he would return to her one day. That he had been hurt and was in hospital, or had perhaps lost his memory, but one day they would be reunited. She did not realise she had been hoping for it until Uncle Arthur spoke and threw any chance of hope away, and Elizabeth lost her breath from the harshness of the blow.

"How could you do this?" she said, her voice shaking with fury. "How could you hide this from me?"

Before her uncle could reply, the door to his study flew open, and a man that Elizabeth did not recognise burst into the room. "Boss!" he said. "The job went south. Patrick's been arrested."

Elizabeth gaped at him, struggling to process his words. Then, with Uncle Arthur shouting after her to stop, she turned and ran from the house.

# CHAPTER 15

$\mathcal{E}$lizabeth knew exactly where the police station was. She had passed it many times in her life, and each time she had eyed it warily, knowing it contained the people who refused to help her mother, failed to protect her father, but would happily hurt a man like Joey for the simple crime of being too poor to eat.

But now her legs flew, her hair tumbling out of its pins, her cloak forgotten despite the winter chill, as she ran across the city. If the police of Birmingham could not be trusted, then that was even *more* reason why she had to get there as fast as she could. She had to help Patrick somehow.

She skidded around the corner of the station in time to see Patrick being dragged up the front steps with his hands locked behind his back. He had a cut above one eye, and he was stumbling slightly as he walked, but he was alive, at least, and whole.

"Patrick!" she shouted. Patrick looked up, startled, and a look of great shame spread over him as he saw the cloakless, almost wild-looking Elizabeth still running toward him.

"Please!" she shouted to the officer who was still dragging him along. "Please, he's not the one responsible."

"I'm going to need to ask you to calm down, miss," the officer said, with barely a glance at her. "We're carrying out important business under the remit of Her Majesty the Queen."

"Please," she said again. She ran up the steps after them, almost stumbling in her haste. Patrick hung his head, unable to risk meeting her eyes. "I need to talk to him. I just need to talk to him, *please.*" She put a hand on the officer's arm, and he shoved her away roughly, causing her to slip back a step.

"Hey!" Patrick said. "She's just a girl."

"A girl associated with the likes of you," the officer mumbled. He turned back to Elizabeth. "Keep shouting, miss, and I'll arrest you for conspiracy with this one."

"All right," she said desperately. "Do it. I just need to talk to him."

"Elizabeth, *no,*" Patrick said, but Elizabeth's heart and mind were both already decided. She would not allow her Uncle Arthur to ruin anyone else's life. She *had* to find a way to help Patrick, and if that meant being arrested too, then so be it.

The officer holding Patrick nodded to another man, who stepped forward and gently took hold of Elizabeth's arm. He was less gentle as he began to drag her up the steps toward the station entrance, but he stopped when another sudden shout rang down the street.

"Wait!" It was Uncle Arthur. He strode toward the scene, his face a little pale, but with a determined set to his chin. "Please, don't arrest either of them. I can sort this out. I have all the answers you need, officers."

Elizabeth gaped at him. Arthur's gaze flickered to Elizabeth, and then to Patrick, before he refocussed on the officers again. "I promise you," he said. "I'm the one you want."

The officers nodded at one another, and the one holding Elizabeth released her and strode over to Uncle Arthur instead. Uncle Arthur did not struggle as they led him up the stairs into the station, along with Patrick. Elizabeth hurried after them.

The officers would not allow Elizabeth to follow Patrick and Uncle Arthur into whatever discussion they were about to have, so she remained in the entrance hall, pacing back and forth until an officer snapped at her to be still, and then sitting in a chair, counting the minutes until an answer might come.

It was a long time before Patrick emerged from inside the station. He looked pale and in shock, but he was not in handcuffs, and no officer held him. Elizabeth ran across the hall to his side and threw her arms around him. "Patrick," she said, pulling back and looking him in the eye. "What happened?"

"Your uncle confessed to everything," he said, sounding in complete shock. "He told them—he told them he was in charge of everything that happened, that I had no idea what I was involved with when I went down there today, that I thought I was just his apprentice, and—and he said, if they let me go, he would confess to everything and help them catch some of the other people involved too."

Elizabeth stared at him. Her uncle had truly given himself up to save Patrick? "And you..." She trailed off, not knowing what she could possibly say.

"They let me go," he said. He rested a hand on Elizabeth's shoulder. "Elizabeth, I know there is no possible way for me to make amends for hiding this from you. But I am incredibly sorry for what we've put you through."

Elizabeth smiled sadly at him. "Let's talk more when we get home," she said. "First, I—I have to speak to Uncle Arthur. If they'll let me."

In truth, she expected little from the officers who had watched her worry for the past couple of hours, but one of the gentlemen, an older man with a heavy walrus moustache, seemed to take pity on her, and merely nodded at her request, leading her through the door into the station proper and then guiding her toward the cells at the rear of the building.

"I must warn you, miss," he said gruffly. "This is no place for a lady."

"He is my uncle," she said firmly. "I need answers from him, no matter where he is."

The officer nodded, and guided Elizabeth down a corridor of mostly empty cells, stopping in front of the bars of one. Uncle Arthur sat on a wooden bench in the otherwise empty room, looking utterly out of place with his fine clothes and neatly groomed beard. He looked up when he heard Elizabeth and the officer approach, and then he winced.

"Please, Elizabeth," he said. "You shouldn't be here."

"Five minutes," the officer said. "Don't try anything funny, either of you. I'll be at the end of the hall."

Elizabeth gave him a wavering smile and watched him retreat before turning back to her uncle. He had stood up and was standing just out of arm's reach. He took in Elizabeth's appearance with wide eyes. "Are you all right?" he asked her. "Are you hurt?"

"No," she said. "I mean, yes, I'm all right. I'm not hurt. Except —I don't understand, Uncle. Why did you do it? Why did you hand yourself over like that?"

"Patrick does not deserve to suffer for my mistakes," he said, "and neither do you. I've ruined so many lives, and for what? Money? Comfort? I live in fear of the people I care about being killed because of my work, and I feel I cannot turn away, or they will be harmed in retribution. I made foolish, selfish choices as a young man that brought us all here today, and I should be the one to pay the price of that. Not Patrick. Not you."

"You weren't there," she whispered. "Whatever Patrick was doing, you weren't there."

"But I sent him there," he said. "I took him as my apprentice, knowing the work was unsavoury and might cause trouble for the lad. I made excuses, saying I was giving him a new life, saving him from the orphanage, but that was no justification. I could have easily taken the boy in without involving him in such terrible things. And you, Elizabeth." He reached through the bars, and Elizabeth took his hand. "You are so brave, and so kind. You did not deserve any of this. I cannot bring back your parents, or your father's shop, or anything that you have lost. But I can ensure that you do not lose any more."

"I'm losing you," Elizabeth said, with tears in her eyes.

"You deserve better, Elizabeth," he said. "You deserve to be free of all this." He squeezed her hand. "Patrick is a good lad. He has a good heart, like yours. I know you will take care of each other."

"But what will happen to you?" Elizabeth asked.

"What I deserve," he said. "Years locked away cannot undo my actions, or the terrible things I have caused, but it is a beginning. I've wanted to tell you, Elizabeth. I have wanted to make amends. But I knew if I told you, you would leave, and then I would be completely unable to protect you from men like me. From men *worse* than me. But I know I've done a great wrong."

Elizabeth opened her mouth to reply, but the officer interrupted her. "That's five minutes, now," he said. "Come along, miss, or you'll be getting me in trouble."

"Take care of yourself, Elizabeth," Uncle Arthur said, squeezing her hand again. "Live the life that you deserve."

Elizabeth did not know what she could possibly say in return, so she simply squeezed his hand back, and gave him a look that she hoped conveyed that she at least partly understood.

# CHAPTER 16

*E*lizabeth and Patrick walked back to Uncle Arthur's house in silence. Patrick seemed almost afraid to speak, of what Elizabeth might say; and Elizabeth's head was too full of thoughts and her heart too full of pain to express anything out loud. The December afternoon was clear and cold, and Elizabeth watched the way her breath clouded in the air before her, thinking about the fragility of everything around them.

They returned home to find Miss Dawn in a fit of worry. "What has happened?" she cried, as soon as they stepped through the door. "Miss Elizabeth running out, and then the master after her."

"The master has been arrested, Miss Dawn," Patrick said. Miss Dawn gasped in shock, and sank into a chair, holding her heart, as Patrick explained what had occurred.

"The master, a criminal?" Miss Dawn said. "And pulling you into that dangerous world as well? Oh, what was he *thinking*? I'm only glad that you are unhurt, Miss Elizabeth. But the master, doing such things?" She shook her head. "Well, what will become of us now?"

Elizabeth heart sank. She had been so wrapped up in the shock of the day's revelations that she had not considered that something must come *after*. A future without Uncle Arthur or Patrick's income, the likely loss of the house as a criminal asset, the breakup of their forged family. She threw her arms around Miss Dawn, and the older woman held her close.

"Don't fret, Miss Elizabeth," she said softly. "We will think of something."

Miss Dawn bustled off to prepare a meal for them all, murmuring about the young ones needing to eat and keep up their strength, and Elizabeth and Patrick were left standing together in the entrance hall. Elizabeth was at a complete loss over what to say.

"She is right," Patrick said softly. "Things will get difficult now."

"Why?" Elizabeth said, his statement barely even registering in her mind. "Why did you do it, Patrick? Why did you join my uncle like this?"

He looked down at the floor. "I told you once that I was an orphan when I met the master," he said. "Seven years old, always hungry, with no family. When Mr. Taylor came looking for an apprentice, I was delighted when he picked me. It felt like a dream. To live in a house like this, where there was always food, and wood for the fire, and people were kind... I would have thought it impossible before I met him. And in the beginning, he kept me far away from the unsavoury elements of his business, just as he's kept you away. I accompanied him to places and I did odd jobs for him, and I was happy. But as I grew older, I wanted to get more involved in his work. I wanted to help, to ensure I was earning my place." He shook his head. "It happened gradually. I knew it was wrong, but—the master gave me so much. And I trusted him. If he said it needed to be done, then I believed it needed to be done." He looked up at Elizabeth, his eyes pleading. "I still don't think he is a bad man, Elizabeth," he said. "He saved me. He could have left me to take the punishment and continued living his life as a free man, but he gave himself to the police instead. I believe he really does care."

"I believe that too," Elizabeth said. But that did not erase the pain of what he had done.

"I cannot entirely regret it," Patrick said softly. "If I had never been associated with your Uncle Arthur, I would never have met you."

Elizabeth gasped at the quiet honesty of his words, but before she could think what to say in response, Patrick was nodding and walking away.

THE HOUSE FELT TOO quiet and empty without Uncle Arthur's presence. Elizabeth did not feel comfortable using the money that Uncle Arthur had left behind, but they needed to eat and pay the rent somehow, and no-one in the household had resources of their own. Elizabeth contemplated selling her skills as a seamstress, and Patrick had the skill for any number of odd jobs, but both were reluctant to establish a new routine in Birmingham after what had occurred. There seemed to be an unspoken agreement in the household that they were all remaining while Uncle Arthur was tried. Once he was found guilty—as he surely would be, given his own determination to confess—they all believed that they would scatter.

Elizabeth, for her part, began dreaming of London again. It would be painful to leave the city she grew up in and all the memories of her family that it held, but she felt she needed a new start, without the spectre of gang violence and police corruption hanging over everything.

The main problem, other than money, she thought, was that she did not want to imagine this "new start" without Patrick beside her. But since the events at the police station, Patrick had been avoiding her, even more than usual. Despite his declaration that he was glad to have met her, Elizabeth would not blame him if he wished to leave everything that reminded him of her Uncle Arthur behind. Of course, that would include her.

But as the days passed, and Patrick offered her little more than polite bows and mumbled greetings whenever he saw her, Elizabeth began to feel slightly desperate. She had already lost so much. Every parental figure in her life was gone. Patrick had been part of her world, in one way or another, since she was seven years' old, and what had initially been little more than childish intrigue had grown over their acquaintance into a heart-deep appreciation for his kindness and a need to see his smile. He felt like one of the few steady things remaining in her life, and she could not bear to lose him.

So, one day, about two weeks after Uncle Arthur's arrest, Elizabeth screwed up her courage and went to find Patrick in the study.

"Miss Elizabeth," he said, startled, when he saw her. "Is something the matter?"

"No," she said. "I'm all right, Patrick. I just—I hoped that I might talk to you. Perhaps we could visit the garden that you showed me before?"

Patrick stared at her for a moment, looking stunned. Then he nodded. "Of course," he said. "It would be my pleasure."

They walked along the street side by side, not speaking or touching. Patrick opened the gate into the garden, and Elizabeth gasped once again at the sight that awaited them. The leaves had all fallen from the trees, leaving spiky, frost-limned branches, and the flowers she had seen before were all gone, leaving empty rose bushes in their wake. But small yellow flowers Elizabeth could not name grew around the bases of the trees, and purple and yellow pansies bloomed in clusters in spots that had previously been bare. The year was coming to a close, and the garden felt like it was resting, awaiting the spring, yet still these bursts of colour and life remained.

Elizabeth wandered over to the fountain under the oak tree and looked at the falling water, working up the courage to speak again. "Patrick," she said softly, after a while. He looked at her without a word, his expression caring, waiting for her to continue. "I hope you know that—" She trailed off, struggling to find the words. "You told me before that you were glad you had met me, despite all that has happened," she said. "And when we were last here, I believe—I thought perhaps you wished to kiss me. But in the past few weeks, I fear that you've been avoiding me, and it breaks my heart not to know why. I understand if you want to leave everything related to my uncle behind, to forget all about him and me. But if there is any chance that you would still like me to be in your life, after all this is over, I—I wanted to ensure you knew that I would like you to be in my life. Very much."

Patrick nodded, and Elizabeth suddenly felt foolish. "But of course," she said quickly, "I understand that things are complicated, and there are many young ladies in the world who are far less trouble than I am, but perhaps, I hoped—"

Patrick cut her off with a kiss. It was a sweet gesture, a simple press of his lips against hers, but Elizabeth gasped, stunned into silence. Her lips tingled as he pulled away again, smiling softly.

"Does—does that mean...?" she asked.

"Elizabeth," he said. "I have wanted you in my life from the moment I first saw you. *I* am the one who doesn't deserve you. I thought I would lose you forever once you learned the truth. I probably still should."

Elizabeth shook her head, unable to look away from his eyes. "I don't want to lose you," she said.

He pressed his hand to her cheek, his thumb tracing the curve beneath her jaw. "I don't want to lose you either."

"Then don't," she said.

"I don't—" he stumbled over the words, "I don't want to be too forward, but—do you mean you would consider marrying me, Elizabeth?"

She laughed softly, her heart bursting with joy. "Yes," she said, and she pressed up onto her tiptoes to kiss him again. "I will marry you."

# CHAPTER 17

*M*iss Dawn was delighted when they told her the news. She hugged both of them, and then bustled away while dabbing at her eyes, murmuring something about making "a proper meal to celebrate."

The three of them were there in court on the day that Uncle Arthur pled guilty for all his crimes and was sentenced to prison. Despite all the pain that he had caused her, Elizabeth found herself crying at the verdict, but Uncle Arthur seemed perfectly at peace as they led him away. Perhaps, she thought, this would help him to resolve the pain and guilt in his heart and allow him to truly become the warm and kind-hearted person she knew him in truth to be.

She and Patrick got married in a small ceremony, with only Miss Dawn there to witness, and then began the process of moving to London for a fresh start, and to finally fulfil Elizabeth's dream.

Although they could no longer afford to employ Miss Dawn, she chose to move to London with them, too, declaring them the only family she knew or wanted. Elizabeth quickly established a reputation as an excellent seamstress, and although her work began as simple mending done by the fireplace in their small new home, she quickly found enough customers to rent her own shop. Miss Dawn assisted with the sewing, while Patrick decided to dedicate himself to the art of button making. His intricately carved wooden designs became very popular, and he often received more orders and requests than he could possibly complete.

After several months, Elizabeth wrote her first letter to Uncle Arthur, and then her second. Uncle Arthur was not always able to reply to her words, but the replies she did receive expressed great joy at hearing any piece of news and suggested that his heart was gradually beginning to heal. Once he was released from prison, Elizabeth thought, perhaps he might come to London to live with them again. It made her smile to imagine Uncle Arthur working as Patrick's apprentice, learning to carve the buttons that were so in demand.

Although they were not rich by any stretch of the imagination, they lived comfortably, and, most importantly, they lived together, sharing their joys and supporting one another through the dark times.

# THE LOST ORPHAN'S CAUSE

## THE LOST ORPHANS OF DARK STREETS:
## PART II

# CHAPTER 1

Nine-year-old Molly had lived in the workhouse for as long as she could remember. She had no last name, because no one at the workhouse had bothered to keep a record of what it was supposed to be. Her mother had died not long after arriving at the workhouse, and Molly had been removed from the women's wing, where she had been allowed to sleep due to her very young age, and sent to the children's wing where she was told she belonged. She could not even be certain that *Molly* was the name her mother had given her. Anyone might have decided on it, and Molly would never know. She could not even remember her mamma.

They were all under the care of Mrs Snorleigh, a plump woman in her fifties who seemed to detest children even more than she detested laziness. Mrs Snorleigh was not a woman to turn to for comfort or sympathy, any more than she was a woman to turn to for fairness and justice. She would have preferred to never be bothered by the children or their concerns, but since that was impossible, she delegated work to her goons when she could, and took out her displeasure on her charges when she could not.

Molly was short and skinny for her age, having spent all her early years working hard and eating workhouse gruel. She was quiet, too, but she was not shy. She had learned to be observant in her years in the workhouse, and as a child with almost nothing to lose, she did not hesitate to speak up for herself or for others when she thought injustice was being done.

One of Molly's earliest memories was shouting at the top of her lungs at one of Mrs Snoreleigh's goons, demanding that he give another girl more food for dinner. Molly's vocabulary hadn't developed enough at the age of four to able to tell the goon that it was obvious that the girl was on the edge of consciousness due to being starved, but she made her message very clear with her high-pitched, shrill screams. The goon tried to shut her up by screaming back, but that didn't stop Molly. In the end, Mrs Snorleigh had to lock Molly in a closest for the night to stop her screaming. Molly had found herself locked in that closet many more times over the past five years.

Molly's stubbornness when it came to justice inevitably led to greater injustice—a beating, extra work, going to bed without supper—but this was never enough to prevent Molly from speaking out again the next time she saw unfairness or cruelty. Molly had a true heart, unbreakably honest and deeply kind, and the definitions of right and wrong were clear as a bell to her. She could not waver, not even if she had wished to.

New children came to the workhouse almost every week, and Molly felt sorry for them, because this was surely the worst workhouse in all of London, if not the whole world. Some of them arrived kicking and screaming, having been brought in off the streets, while others sniffed and cried for parents that had been sent to their own wings of the workhouse and were unlikely to return.

A new girl had recently joined the workhouse. She was around Molly's age, but like many of the girls there, she was a meek, quiet thing, seeming to strive to be noticed as little as possible.

Molly found herself sleeping next to this new girl on her first night in the workhouse. It didn't surprise Molly when she heard stifled sobs. Many of the girls cried during the night, and even Molly herself cried sometimes, especially when she thought about the mother she couldn't remember.

Molly wished she could comfort the new girl, but she did not know what she could say. The workhouse was a terrible place, and once children were separated from their parents, they rarely ever saw them again. What could Molly say to make any of that feel better than it truly was, without lying to the girl? Still, Molly kept an eye on her, determined to help her if she could.

"Am I going to be okay?" The new girl sobbed quietly. Was she talking to Molly, or just out into the night? Molly couldn't tell. "I miss my mama."

Molly didn't want to lie to her and say she would see her mama again. She knew it was almost certain this girl would never see any of her family ever again. So, she said nothing, only placing her small hand on top of the girl's.

Not two days passed after the new girl arrived at the workhouse before Molly found herself needed. After eating a breakfast of thin gruel in the large, cold children's hall, the girls filed off to begin their work for the day. The girls under the age of ten generally went to a narrow, dimly lit room, where they sewed buttons onto shirts and dresses. It was fiddly work, and they were watched over by Mrs Snorleigh's goons, who were there to 'encourage' them to work faster. If they did not sew on enough buttons by sundown, dinner would be forfeit. Molly often pricked her finger with the needle—not enough to bleed, but enough to hurt. Soon, when she turned ten, she would be moved to join the older girls, who sewed all kinds of clothes, shirts, dresses, uniforms and anything else that was required.

The first problem came that morning when the new girl walked the wrong way after breakfast. She was stumbling along, looking down at her feet, following the girl in front of her, but when the corridor split, and the older girl went left to the general sewing room, the new girl continued to stumble after her.

"Oi!" one of Mrs Snorleigh's goons shouted. "Where d'ya think you're going, girlie?"

The new girl jumped, her face turning white with fright. She looked about in panicked confusion as the girl she had been following walked on without so much as a backward glance to see what had happened.

Molly darted forward and took the new girl by the hand before the goon could get any closer. "This way," she whispered to her, and tugged on her arm for the new girl to follow. The girl stumbled after her without any resistance. "My name's Molly," Molly whispered.

The girl blinked. "I'm Susan," she said.

"No talking!" the goon shouted. Molly screwed up her nose, but he did not notice, and the two girls fell silent.

Molly ended up working beside Susan on the long table that day. Piles of shirts waited in several baskets. Their task was to sew all the necessary buttons onto the cloth, and then deposit them in a different basket for whatever came next. If they worked through all the shirts, more work would be found for them. If they failed to complete the task, they would go without supper.

Susan kept her eyes focused on her work, but it was clear, from the few glances that Molly stole at her, that she had hardly ever sewn anything in her life before. Her movements were clumsy and unsure, and her buttons were loose, with trailing threads.

"Pull the thread tighter," Molly hissed to her.

"Shut it!" the goon watching them yelled.

Susan jumped and returned to her work with renewed speed. As she fed the needle through the cloth, her finger slipped, and she let out a gasp of pain. Molly watched in horror as blood beaded on the pad of Susan's fingertip and fell to stain the off-white shirt beneath.

Mrs Snorleigh's goon must have been watching closely, because he was behind her in a moment, his meaty hand clutching Susan's shoulder and hauling her backwards.

"You clumsy idiot!" he shouted. "You think people want to pay for shirts with a filthy orphan's blood on them? You've ruined it!"

"I—I didn't mean to," Susan said. Her face had turned white, and she was shaking with fear.

"You think this is a game, girlie?" the goon spat. All around her, the other girls bent over their work, determinedly not looking at the scene that was unfolding. His fingers dug into her shoulder, gripping so tightly that it must have hurt. He shook her. "You're here out of the goodness of our hearts, instead of out on the streets where you should be, and look at this. Look at it!"

"Leave her alone!" Molly shouted. Her cry echoed, but the man ignored her. He continued to shake Susan.

"Do you think that's good enough?" he asked her. "Do ya?"

Susan shook her head. Tears splashed down her cheeks.

"Leave her alone!" Molly shouted again. Mrs Snorleigh's goons were always cruel, but it felt particularly unjust for them to focus on such a new and lost-looking girl. Did they not have an ounce of sympathy or honour in their tiny shrivelled hearts? Susan was trembling with fear, tears rolling down her cheeks, and Molly could not bear it.

She picked up a plank of wood that had been leant against the wall. It was heavy and difficult to lift, but Molly was driven on by her anger. She raised the plank and hit the man with it. She aimed to hit his head, but she was not quite tall enough, so the plank collided with his neck and shoulder instead.

The man released Susan and turned on Molly. "You filthy brat!" he cried. "You'll pay for that!" He gripped her arm now, tightly enough to bruise.

Molly did not expect Susan to speak out in her defence, so she was not disappointed when the other girl did not. She just stared in teary-eyed fright as the goon dragged Molly roughly out of the room.

The goon said nothing more, but Molly knew she was being taken to Mrs Snorleigh for punishment. Molly quivered with the injustice of it all.

"What is going on?" Mrs Snorleigh asked, as the goon dragged Molly into her room.

"This one has been causing trouble," the goon said. "She attacked me with a piece of wood!"

Mrs Snorleigh had a round face, but it was not a kind one. She peered down at Molly through narrowed eyes. "Well?" she asked sharply. "What do you have to say for yourself, girl?"

"He was hurting Susan!" Molly said. "He was shouting at her!"

"And I fair bet Susan deserved it, just as much as you do," Mrs Snorleigh replied. "Ungrateful child! Do you know how lucky you are to be here? You would be starving out on the streets without our charity."

"I'm starving here!" Molly replied.

Mrs Snorleigh stepped forward and slapped Molly about the face. "You don't know what starvation is, girl," she said. "You are *blessed* to have a roof over your head, a place to sleep, a place to work. You receive all these from the goodness of our queen and our government, and if you ask me, you don't deserve a scrap of it. Yet here you are. You would be dead without this charity. Show a little gratitude."

"No!" Molly cried. Her face stung where Mrs Snorleigh had

struck it, and the goon was twisting her arm painfully. It was all so *unfair*. How were they allowed to treat the children like this and call it charity? "I'd rather be out on the streets than being stuck here with you!"

"Spoiled brat," Mrs Snorleigh hissed. "Jackson," she said to the goon. "Take her out to the yard and teach her some gratitude. It will have to be a particularly harsh lesson, I fear."

"O'course, ma'am," the goon named Jackson said. "Right away. Come on, you." He tightened his grip on Molly's arm and dragged her out of the room again.

Molly was shaking. But it was anger, she told herself, *not* fear. She wouldn't give them the satisfaction of being afraid. But when Jackson pulled her through a door and into the cold, ice-rimed yard, she began to shake all the more fiercely. The yard was empty, and far across it, Molly could see the iron gates of the workhouse, gates she could never remember passing through in her entire life. They stood ajar, unlocked. The entire world waited beyond them.

Jackson released her arm and picked up a short plank of wood that had been discarded in the yard. "We'll see how you like it, shall we?" he said, with a slight grin. The plank looked heavy to Molly, dangerously so. One whack with it would cause her bruising, for certain. A full beating would probably leave her struggling to walk or eat.

Now she was definitely shaking with fear.

Jackson reached to grab her again, but Molly ducked away and started to run. "Oi!" Jackson shouted. She heard him begin to chase after her, and she ran as fast as she could for the gate. It wasn't too far. She could make it. And if he caught her....

She reached the gate. Up close, she could see that the workhouse gates actually were locked, fastened with a padlock and chain, but the chain allowed them to open just enough for a small child to slip through. If she could just make it.

She felt a burning sensation across her scalp as Jackson

grabbed her by the hair and pulled her back, throwing her hard against the ground. A grunt escaped her mouth.

"You just don't learn your lesson, do ya?" Jackson was no longer grinning. A dark and terrifying expression was firmly planted on his face now. He raised the plank yet again. "Now, let's try this again, shall we?"

MOLLY COULD BARELY SIT down after the beating Jackson gave her, and she had let out a squeal she quickly stifled the next morning when she sat down to do her work. She held back the tears, as the already uncomfortable stools now were an unending source of pain. From the corner of her eye, Molly could see Jackson prowling around, that grin on his face yet again. Molly wouldn't let herself give him the satisfaction of seeing her cry out in pain, and she used all of her determination to keep a blank facial expression. The pain was excruciating though.

But now she knew about the gate. Now she knew how she would escape this place.

It would take at least another month before Molly would be in any state to make another attempt at getting through the gate, as she would need to be even faster than she was before. Right now, the best she could do was a waddle slower than even her normal walking speed. Molly would have to bind her time and wait.

Molly waited. The workhouse didn't get any better for her, but the thought and dream of escape made everything easier to shoulder, as she knew it would all be over soon. Every day, she would wake up and check how it felt to walk, and whenever possible, which wasn't very often, how it felt to run. She felt her muscles healing, and her strength returning. And as she went to bed almost four weeks after the beating with the wooden plank,

Molly knew that the next day would be the day she would escape this place and get as far away from it as she could.

The next morning, Molly put her plan into action. As the girls where being served their meagre breakfast, Molly kept her eye out for Jackson. As soon as she spotted him, she made her way over to him, her bowl of gruel in hand. As she came near him, she purposefully tripped up, and sent the questionably coloured substance all over Jackson's face and clothes. Jackson roared out in frustration.

"Come here you!" Jackson raged, as he grabbed Molly by the arm. Molly didn't resist as Jackson dragged her. He was taking her exactly where she wanted to go. Outside.

Molly spied the gate, and the chain that allowed it to open just enough for someone as small as her to slip through. Jackson hadn't thought to fix it. Maybe he hadn't even noticed the gap. Molly's heart was beating so loud she could feel it in her ears. This was her last chance. If she was caught again this time, she was sure Jackson wouldn't let her off with just a beating. She would have to pick the exact right moment to run.

"What have I said about you and learning lessons, girl?" Jackson began searching around for something to deliver the punishment. "We keep trying to teach you respect, and you keep disrepectin' me and Mrs. Snoreleigh." Molly saw his eyes maliciously brighten when he spotted a broom propped up against the wall. He began to stride over to it. That's when Molly made her move.

She ran faster than she ever thought she could. Tearing her way to the gate. Jackson had his back to her at first and missed her jumping up. He spun his head round rapidly and let out a cry. "Get back here!"

Molly felt the phantom pain from her first escape attempt. Her scalp tingling. This just pushed her on to run faster. The gate was right there. She reached it this time and slipped herself through.

Jackson gave out a bellow of rage as he reached the gate a second behind her and tried to grab the back of her dress through the gap. She slipped out of his grip and ran.

"You'll starve, girl!" Jackson shouted after her. A few strangers turned to look, but nobody tried to stop her. "You'll freeze to death in a day out there. You'll be back. But not if you know what's good for you!"

Molly did not look back. All she knew was that she had to get as far away from here as she possibly could.

# CHAPTER 2

*M*olly raced through the streets of London with no destination in mind. She did not know the world outside the workhouse gates, so she had no idea where she was or where she might be going. All the streets looked the same. Many were crowded with people and horses, and they all smelled terrible. Molly did not slow down to take in the details. She wove through the crowd, not stopping for people's surprised gasps, nor for the barking of dogs or insults shouted by other children. She felt that if she stopped running, she would never start again. The goon's words would prove true, and she would end up back at the workhouse, never to leave it again, so she ran and ran.

After a while, she could not have returned to the workhouse even if she wished to. She was utterly lost in the city's winding streets. Everything was unfamiliar. The sun was beginning to set, and men with long poles were walking around and lighting the streetlamps. The crowds of people thinned, and the city grew quieter.

Molly finally collapsed to a stop and fought for her breath. She had a painful stitch in her side, and although she was warm from running, she shivered as the icy wind blew around her. She was not even wearing a cloak.

The seconds ticked past, and Molly's adrenaline faded, the reality of her situation sinking in. Her stomach ached from hunger, and her throat was painfully dry from thirst. Her limbs ached, and the world seemed hazy around her. She had run and run until she had no energy left inside her, and then she had continued after that. She tried to take another step forward, and she stumbled.

Molly blinked at the dirty cobblestone beneath her hand, unable to understand how it had ended up so close. Had she fallen? Then she heard a voice, shouting to her as though from very far away. She blinked again and looked up to see another girl about her age looking down at her. The girl was covered in dirt, and her long hair was unkempt and untied, but her wide eyes were filled with concern. `

Then a man stepped into view. Molly's vision swam. She could not make out the details of him, except that he had a raggedy beard and wore a beat-up top hat. He smiled at her, and Molly fell into unconsciousness.

WHEN MOLLY AWOKE SOMETIME LATER, her first feeling was one of panic. She recalled Mrs Snorleigh's punishment, the goon's grip on her arm, and then the feeling of running and running and running, knowing she could not stop for any reason, no matter how tired she became.

Why had she stopped? Molly could not remember. She thought perhaps she had fallen. Then she remembered seeing a girl's face, and a raggedy man. She sat up suddenly and opened her eyes. She was lying on blankets in a small, unfamiliar hovel, and terror raced through Molly. She had not gotten here by herself.

"'s all right," a soft voice said behind her. "Don't be scared. 'm glad you're awake."

Molly looked to her left. The unkempt girl from the street was sitting beside her. She held out a cup of water, and Molly took it and drank it down greedily. The girl had a heel of bread too, and when she handed it to Molly, Molly ate it in three bites. It was old and stale—and some of the best food Molly had ever tasted.

"M'name's Hazel," the girl said. "What's yours?"

"Molly," Molly said. She considered the girl beside her again. It was a little like staring at her reflection in water. The girl had the same round face as Molly, the same thick brown hair and brown eyes, although her nose was different from Molly's, and she was taller and seemed better fed. "Where am I?" Molly asked her.

"Don't worry," Hazel said. "You're safe here. This is Haven."

"Haven?" Molly repeated, and Hazel nodded, smiling.

"That's right," she said. "It's sort of a family. There are lots of people here like me and you."

"Children?" Molly asked.

"Beggars," Hazel said. "If you wait, my pa—he can explain it better than me." She looked behind her and shouted. "Pa! Pa, she's awake!"

Molly heard footsteps, and the raggedy man she'd seen on the street before appeared. He had taken off his beat-up top hat, but he was still dressed in a once-fine coat that was now covered in holes and patches. His brown hair and beard were unkempt and streaked with grey, and he wore woolen gloves with holes at the fingertips. In her panic when she was running, Molly might have thought he was a frightening figure, but Molly knew the look of someone who planned to do you harm by now. This man had a kind face behind his wild beard, and his eyes were gentle and understanding. This was a good person, she thought. Someone she could trust.

"Glad to see you up and about," the man said. "We were a bit worried about you. What's your name, love?"

"Molly," Molly said again.

"I'm Cuthbert," the man said, "but that's a silly name, so everyone calls me Boots." He smiled. "That's a silly name too, I reckon, but it suits me better, don't you think? You gave us a scare there, Molly. 's lucky my Hazel found you. Where were you running from?"

"The workhouse," Molly whispered. "But please. Don't make me go back there. You can't!"

"Hey, now," Boots said. "Steady. We're not going to make you go anywhere you don't want to. Especially nowhere that set you off running like that. Just checking if anyone might be chasing after you. But the workhouse—I think you're safe from it now. You can stay here as long as you like."

"In Haven?" Molly asked.

"Hazel told you about that, did she?" Boots asked. "Yeah, we take all sorts here. We're a bit of a family, though maybe not like the kind those rich folk have. A better kind, I think. Come on. If you're feeling better, we'll show you around."

Hazel beamed at Molly and held out a hand. Molly took it.

"That was my room," Hazel said, as she led Molly out. "But you can share it with me if you want, if you stay. I've always wanted a sister my age! There aren't many girls here, and they're all older than me."

Out in the main room, Molly saw several other children and young adults sitting about. Two boys who looked about fifteen were playing a game flipping tokens with their fingers, while an older girl was stirring a pot over the fire.

"You're awake!" the older girl said. "Stew'll be ready in a few if you're hungry."

"That's Joan," Hazel said. "She's nice."

"I can hear you talking, Hazel," Joan said with a laugh.

"Well, that's why I was nice about you," Hazel said. She stuck her tongue out at the older girl, and Joan stuck her tongue out back at her.

One of the boys playing the game stood up and strode over. He stuck out his hand for Molly to shake. "'m Jack," he said. "And that's my brother Richard." The other boy gave a grunt of greeting.

"Hey now, don't crowd her, lad," Boots said. "You'll scare her off."

"I'm saying hello!" Jack said. "That's a *nice* thing to do, you know. Polite, like."

"There are others as well," Hazel said. "Not here at the moment, though."

"People are free to come and go as they like," Boots said. "This ain't a prison. You want somewhere safe to sleep and eat, you can stay here. You want to be on your own for a bit, then you can do that too. Still, Timmy and Max should be back soon."

"What do you think?" Hazel asked her with a grin.

"How much does it cost?" Molly asked. "To stay here, I mean."

Boots laughed. "Cost? There's no cost, girl. If you want to stay here as part of the family, then we work together, share our earnings to make sure we all get something to eat. 's nothing more than that. We take care of each other."

Molly liked the sound of that. She had spent her life at the workhouse taking care of others, but she had never really had anyone who might return the favour. She'd told herself that that was all right, that doing what was right was what was important, but secretly she yearned for someone to do right by her as well.

"And what—what's the work that you do?" Molly asked tentatively. Hazel had mentioned something about begging.

"This and that," Boots said. "Some of the money is what's given to us. I reckon you and Hazel would be good at that together. People'll want to give to you. We also relieve some of the richer folk of a few coins here and there. Nothing that they need."

Molly bit her lip. "Isn't that bad?" she asked softly.

"Maybe according to the coppers," Boots said. "But not to anyone you ask with sense. Those rich folks, they have more money than they know what to do with. They don't need it to eat, like we do. And is it right that some people have too much money, while others, like us, don't have near enough to even buy some bread to eat?"

Molly considered his argument. It made sense. The rules said that she should always listen to and obey Mrs Snorleigh, but that had not made Mrs Snorleigh's orders right or just. She lived comfortably, while the children under her care suffered, and she could ask her goons to do anything, even beat a girl with a wooden plank, without any consequences.

Molly bit her lip and nodded, and Boots smiled. "You can stay as long as you like," Boots said. "No worries about that."

Hazel grinned at her. "You're going to stay?" Molly nodded again, and Hazel gave a squeal of delight and threw her arms around her. "We'll be sisters!" she said. "It'll be wonderful. You'll see!"

And Molly could not help but smile and hug her back.

# CHAPTER 3

*I*t did not take long for Haven to feel far more like home than the workhouse ever had. The biggest surprise to Molly was that Boots and the others all seemed to actually *like* having her around. They smiled at her when she came home, and exclaimed in delight at the money she brought in. Molly fell asleep at night cuddled next to Hazel, and for the first time, she drifted off feeling safe, happy and wanted. She had never known family before, but this, she thought, must be what it was like. Life at Haven might not be very conventional, and it might not always be comfortable, but finally Molly felt she had a real place in the world.

The years passed, and Molly could no longer imagine wanting a life away from Boots and Hazel, who truly had become a sister to her. Although at first Molly and Hazel made their contribution by begging, easily gaining donations from passers-by with their large eyes and hungry expressions, she soon discovered that she had an even greater talent. Molly often noticed that the richest looking people never stopped to offer a coin to them, or to anyone else they passed. In fact, the poorer the person passing looked, the more likely they seemed to be to throw what they could Molly and Hazel's way.

Molly hated it. Those who knew what it was to be in need were willing to help others, while those who had never struggled or suffered in their lives strode straight past the poverty on their doorstep without a second thought. Sometimes, Molly tried speaking directly to these people, and they almost always gave her a disgusted, superior sort of look before striding away. Molly didn't think it was right.

So, she asked one of the older boys, Jack, to teach her how to pick pockets. Jack was reluctant at first. "I don't want to be responsible if you get caught," he said. But Molly insisted, and when Boots said that he thought it a good idea, Jack relented.

"She's young and sweet-looking enough, Jack," Boots said. "Even if they catch her, she won't get in much trouble. Best to teach her, or she'll try to do it anyway, and that'll be worse."

Molly was a quick study. She had nimble fingers and a sweet smile, and the two combined allowed her to seize her prize without her mark suspecting a thing. Driven by indignation at their selfishness, she soon started targeting far richer folks than the others often did, undeterred by Jack's warning that the richest marks were usually the most eager to see you punished if you got caught.

Her boldness paid off. The riskiest marks often provided the greatest rewards, and Molly was soon the most successful member of Boots's family, more than earning her keep. She often went out with Hazel to find new marks, but although Hazel tried to keep up with her adopted sister, she lacked some of Molly's confidence, and Molly worried that one day her sister's hesitation might lead to disaster.

By the time Molly was nineteen, she had lost much of the nimbleness that had allowed her to weave between marks as a small child, but her confidence had only grown. She was still skinny for her age, and a fast runner, with an excellent knowledge of London's alleys and hiding places, so she was never too concerned about escaping from trouble, and although she was no longer invisible in the way small children in crowds could often be, her sassy look and knowing smile offered her plenty of opportunities to distract and befuddle her marks.

On this spring day, Molly and Hazel were working together to try to bring in a big haul for Haven. Boots did not have the same energy that he had had ten years ago, and he often complained about pain in his knees. Molly and Hazel were hoping to bring in enough extra money to buy him some medicine and offer him a little relief.

A pair of gentlemen were approaching down the street, and Molly nudged Hazel to get her attention. The men looked to be in their fifties or sixties, with silver hair and well-groomed moustaches, and their clothes suggested more than comfortable wealth. One was talking idly to the other, who was looking at his pocket watch and nodded vaguely in response. They seemed the perfect marks. Any man who showed off such a finely crafted pocket watch must have a decent amount of wealth, and they were distracted enough that they would not notice what was happening until it had already happened. And if they did chase them... well, their portly figures suggested that Molly and Hazel could outrun them without even trying.

Molly shot Hazel a questioning look, and Hazel nodded. They leaned in close together, as though they were two girls sharing a conversation without a care in the world and waited for their marks to approach. Molly could not resist glancing at the watch which the gentleman was now returning to his pocket, but the value of the haul would not be worth the risk. It was fastened to the man's lapel by a chain, and even if she managed to unfasten it, he would almost certainly notice what she had done before she could step away.

She glanced at Hazel again, silently conveying that her sister should go for the man on the left, while she went for the one on the right. Hazel's expression told her that she understood. The pair waited until their marks were almost level with them, and then began to walk forwards, throwing themselves into lively conversation before accidentally colliding with the men.

"Watch where you're going!" one of the men shouted, as Molly stepped back, his coin purse already safely inside her own pocket. Molly began to scurry away, and then turned back when she heard another shout.

Hazel had gone for the pocket watch, but she had not been quick enough. Although she had unclasped the chain and ducked out of arm's reach, the man had noticed her efforts, and now he was bearing down on her.

Hazel was not as fast a runner as Molly, nor as agile, so Molly made a quick decision. "Oi!" she shouted, to get the man's attention, before grabbing the watch from her sister's hand and taking off running.

The men followed the watch, as Molly had hoped they would, allowing Hazel to take off running in the other direction. Molly tore down the street, her heart racing. She could lose these men easily. She barely even really needed to run. And then she heard one of them shout.

"Police! Thief! Stop her!"

From around the corner ahead, Molly heard footsteps and then a shrill whistle. She glanced up just in time to see a policeman running toward her. Of course, it would be her luck that one had been lurking, within earshot but out of sight. She swerved and dove down a side street, but she could hear the policeman following her.

Molly felt giddy as she ran. Part of her was terrified, the risk of getting caught always a frightening thought, but the rest of her was full of excitement. She had been forced to run from the police before, and the danger of it always provided a thrill.

After ten years, she also knew these streets so well that she could have drawn a map of them in the dark. She knew every winding alley, every dead end and surprising escape route, every gateway and lock.

Molly immediately headed for an alley she had used to escape from the police before. At the end, there was an iron gate that could be locked and unlocked from the outside only. Someone small might stick their hand through the bars to unfasten it from the inside—someone like Molly, for example— but it was beyond the abilities of most adults.

Even better, the gate was currently open. Molly tore down the narrow alley and swung past the gate, before turning and slamming it shut. She slid the lock into place as the policeman reached her, and looked up at him with a triumphant grin on her face.

For the first time, she got a good look at her pursuer. She had expected to see a gruff middle-aged man, complete with whiskers and a deeply disapproving expression, but the person who looked back at her could not be much older than Molly herself. He had no whiskers or lines on his face, and a few tufts of brown hair stuck out from underneath his helmet, making it seem more like a costume than a uniform item.

He looked at the now-locked gate and then at her and smiled. "Afternoon, miss," he said. Molly, who had been preparing to turn and run, was so surprised by the mildness in his tone that she stopped and laughed. "Ain't you a little old to be running around the streets, miss?"

"Ain't you a little young to be playing a policeman?" she retorted.

The policeman laughed. "Good thing I'm not playing as one, then." He turned and ran back the way he had come, and Molly quickly gathered her wits and ran on. She turned down one alley, and then another, and then gasped in surprise as she felt firm hands fastening around her wrists.

"What—"

The very same policeman was standing before her, looking

almost apologetic as he began to put her hands in handcuffs. "Sorry, miss," he said. "I know my way around these streets too, you know."

Molly struggled a little, just for the principle of the thing, but she knew it was useless. He'd caught her. Her heart was still pounding from the chase, and she struggled to catch her breath.

"My name's Lawrence Carter, by the way," he said. "What's yours?"

"Molly," she said, without thinking. "Just Molly."

"Well, Just Molly," he said, as he guided her away. "It's a pleasure to make your acquaintance."

"Forgive me if I don't return the sentiment, Mr Carter," she said. "I rather hoped I wouldn't see your face again."

"Aw, now there's a pity," the policeman said. "And a handsome face such as mine as well?"

"You've got a high opinion of yourself, Mr Carter," Molly said.

"Am I wrong, Miss Molly?"

Molly scowled at him and did not reply, and Lawrence laughed again. "Now don't worry, miss," he added. "I'm taking you in now, but I'll keep you safe. Put you in our nicest cell."

"I'm sure I'm much obliged, sir," Molly said, in a mocking voice, but as she spoke, fear struck her as she realised the severity of her situation. She was a criminal, and she had been caught. She might be able to talk her way out of many situations, but she had been caught by the policeman with the stolen goods in hand, after running away from him and taunting him. A nice cell for the meantime was probably the best she could hope for. And she'd heard tales of what could happen to a person when shoved in a crowded cell full of criminals, especially to women. Some policemen made the effort to keep women separate, but others were callous and cruel, and barely saw their catches as human.

At least she felt that Lawrence Carter would not put her at risk.

But she fell quiet as he led her up the steps into the police building. What was he going to do with her? Would she be sent to jail? Or, worse, would they find out where she was from and send her back to a workhouse? Her pride would not allow her to beg or plead with the police, but she felt nauseous and a little dizzy as Lawrence processed her and handed her over to another policeman to be taken to a cell.

At least he kept his word about her accommodations. She had the small cell all to herself, and it was relatively clean and stench-free, for a cell. There was no mattress or chair, which was probably a relief considering what might have taken up residence in such a place, but there was a stone ledge that could serve as either a seat or a bed.

Molly sat down on it and pulled her knees up to her chest. As soon as she was alone, the tears began to fall. Very little frightened Molly, but she was frightened now. Would she ever be able to see her found family again? They would not come for her here. It would put all of the rest of them in far too much danger; it couldn't be risked. And surely the police would not send her on her way again, back to the street gang with their best wishes.

Her life as she had known it was almost certainly over.

Molly curled into a ball and wept.

# CHAPTER 4

$\mathcal{T}$he sound of a key in the cell door pulled Molly out of her misery. She would not let anyone here see her cry. She wiped her eyes with the back of her hand and sat up straight as a figure entered the cell.

It was Lawrence Carter, the policeman who had arrested her. He looked even younger now without his hat on. His hair stuck up at odd angles. It was oddly charming.

He pulled the cell door closed behind him and approached Molly with a bowl in his hands. He offered it to her. It was soup, steaming hot, and the smell of it made Molly's stomach twist with hunger. Still, she did not take it from him.

Lawrence nodded and sat down on the stone bench beside Molly, putting the bowl of soup between them. "Please," he said. "You need to eat."

Molly shot him a suspicious look, but the alluring smell of the hot soup was too much to resist. Throwing dignity aside, Molly seized the bowl and took her first mouthful of soup. She couldn't remember the last time she had eaten something so warm and so warming. They never exactly starved with Boots at Haven, but they didn't feast either, and most food that came their way was either old or cold. This soup tasted delicious.

"So," Lawrence said. "You going to tell me what you're doing out on the streets?"

"Not sure it's your business," Molly replied.

"I think it might be," Lawrence said mildly. "You are sitting in a cell right now. I can help you."

Molly shook her head. "You wouldn't understand."

"I used to live on the streets too," he said. "I understand."

Molly took another mouthful of soup, not looking at him. Even if he had once lived on the streets, he clearly did not now. In fact, he was one of the people looking to make life on the street harder. She couldn't trust him.

After a moment, Lawrence shook his head. "What about that girl with you?"

"What girl?" Molly asked, in what she hoped was an innocent voice.

"The girl you helped by distracting me," Lawrence said. "Your sister. Is she your twin?"

Molly snorted and didn't reply.

After a moment, Lawrence rose again. "Well," he said. "Goodnight, then."

She did not speak until he was almost at the cell door. "What's going to happen to me?" she asked.

"There'll be a court case," Lawrence said. "With the evidence we have, I'm afraid you'll most likely be found guilty and imprisoned."

"Only if that man *wants* me imprisoned," Molly said, suddenly angry. "He got his watch back, didn't he?"

"The man you stole from is not the one pursuing prosecution," Lawrence said. "It is a woman named Mrs Snorleigh."

He left the cell before Molly could reply.

∾

MOLLY SPENT the next few days in the cell, with no one for company except Lawrence when he brought her food. She tried to remain aloof around him, but the loneliness soon began to eat at her, and she was too curious about Mrs Snorleigh to not ask questions. Yet Lawrence could tell her nothing about Mrs Snorleigh's intentions, or how she had even found Molly. Molly was not even certain what the charges against her must be, since she had not stolen the watch from Mrs Snorleigh. Could they be for running away? But she was certain that Mrs Snorleigh did not care about any of her charges and was much happier with Molly gone.

Lawrence had warned her that any resistance would only result in a harsher punishment, so when a different policeman arrived to take Molly to the courtroom, Molly followed him quietly. They passed a few people on their journey, most of whom ignored her. But one well-dressed man in a top hat and a fine coat was talking to a policeman by the entrance, and he froze when his eyes fell on Molly. He watched her, seemingly without blinking, his mouth agape, until Molly's escort steered her around the corner and out of sight. Molly did not know what to make of it, but she had greater concerns now.

The courtroom was small, with only a few people present, including Lawrence standing off to one side, but Molly immediately searched all the faces for the one she had not seen in a decade.

Time had not been kind to Mrs Snorleigh. She looked far more than ten years older than the last time Molly had seen her. Her skin fell in wrinkled folds on her face and neck, and her eyes were beady and squinted. Her hair was grey and patchy in places, and Molly might have struggled to recognise her if not for the familiar, cruel smile plastered on her face.

Molly did not know how court worked, and no one gave her the opportunity to ask. She sat where she was told to sit, and remained quiet, hoping that a meek look might work in her favour. But it was difficult to remain quiet when Mrs Snorleigh began to speak. The woman immediately branded Molly as a troublemaker, a girl without morals, despite the good lessons that Mrs Snorleigh had tried to instill in her.

"Rough and rebellious," Mrs Snorleigh said, "and a thief, even as a small child."

"That's not true!" Molly said. She had broken many unjust rules in the workhouse, but she had never been a thief.

"Even now, she's speaking out of turn," Mrs Snorleigh said. "She fought and bit, and she ran away when we attempted to reprimand her, taking valuable workhouse property with her."

"I didn't take anything!" Molly replied, but Mrs Snorleigh ignored her.

"I'm not surprised she has turned into a fully-fledged criminal," Mrs Snorleigh said. "She always had the temperament for it, even as a small girl."

Molly opened her mouth to reply again but was interrupted by the doors of the courtroom flying open. The well-dressed man from before strode inside, still wearing his top hat. He looked to be in his forties or so, younger than Boots, with a well-trimmed moustache. Fury was etched all over his face.

"Stop this!" he shouted. "I demand you stop this at once. This court case is over."

The judge looked affronted by the interruption. "This is most irregular, sir."

"Indeed it is, my good sir," the man said. "Everything about this situation is irregular, and it must be rectified immediately." Molly glanced at Lawrence, hoping to glean some hint of what was occurring from his expression, but he looked as perplexed as she felt. "My name is Hugo Bennet, and this girl..." Mr Hugo Bennet took a moment to catch his breath. "Is my daughter."

The words were so outlandish that Molly was certain she

must have misheard. But from the gasps and shocked expressions on other people's faces, they had heard the same as she had.

"Nonsense!" Mrs Snorleigh spat. "This child is an orphan. A workhouse wretch!"

"And how did this child come to be at the workhouse?" he asked. "My darling daughter was stolen from me and my wife by ruffians as a baby, and no doubt sold on to a workhouse or some criminal enterprise. Well, ma'am?"

Mrs Snorleigh turned bright red and did not answer.

The judge leaned forward slightly. "Well," he said. "Answer the man."

"She was sold to me," Mrs Snorleigh said. "I admit that. A pair of not-too-fine-looking folk came in and asked for coin for their daughter. O'course, that's not normally in my remit, but these were very suspicious-looking characters. If I didn't take the girl, she'd only end up somewhere terrible. For her own good, I handed over a few coins and took her."

"You told me my mother was in the workhouse with me!" Molly said. "You said she died!"

Mrs Snorleigh ignored her.

"Your honour," Mr Bennet said. He strode forward, pulling a locket out of his pocket. "This is a portrait of my late wife. Compare her look to the girl's. The similarity is striking."

The judge considered the portrait, and then looked at Molly. "It is remarkable," he said.

Molly longed to see the picture, but she did not dare interrupt again. Might it be true? Might she actually have a family? It all seemed so unlikely. Surely this man was pulling a trick of some sort. The question was whether it was a trick played on her, or for her own benefit.

"Please, your honour," Mr Bennet said, "I have longed for my daughter for the past eighteen years. Allow her to return home with me. Any crime she has committed can only be a result of the cruelty she has so unjustly faced."

"Well," the judge said. "I have heard something of your reputation in this city, Mr Bennet, and by all accounts, you are a respectable and upstanding man. It does not strike me as within your character to cause such an ado without the direst of reasons."

"Indeed, it is not, sir," Mr Bennet said. "I caught a glimpse of the girl on her way to the court, and I knew in my heart at once that she was my daughter."

"Very well," the judge said, sounding tired. "The case is a small matter either way, and if you are to vouch for the girl's housing and rehabilitation, then a little financial compensation to the man whose watch was stolen is all that will be required."

Molly felt numb. The judge was actually agreeing with the man. He was vouching for him. Why would a well-to-do man like this claim a street rat like her, unless he truly believed himself to be her father? But how could that be possible? Molly did not have family by blood. She had never had family by blood.

"Child," the judge said to Molly, his expression much kinder than it had been before. "This must be rather sudden, but I can vouch for Mr Bennet being a good man. If it is your wish, you may depart with him."

"If it is my wish?" Molly repeated in a whisper. "What is my alternative?"

"Mrs Snorleigh here takes responsibility for you," he says, "and, I assume, the trial continues."

Molly's legs shook beneath her. She looked at Mr Bennet again. He had a kind face, and at that moment it was full of hope and joy. Molly could not imagine that any man could fake such an expression. He truly believed in what he was claiming. He thought her his long-lost daughter.

He would be disappointed, she thought, when he realised

that he was mistaken. Molly did not wish to deceive him. But it was possible that he was correct, wasn't it? And her alternatives were unbearable. Would it really hurt, to try it and see?

"I—I would be happy to go with Mr Bennet," she said, stumbling slightly over her words. "If that is—if—"

"Excellent," the judge said, cutting Molly off with a bang of his gavel. "It is settled. Case dismissed."

The policeman who had led Molly into the courtroom now began to lead her out of it, toward where Mr Bennet waited. Mr Bennet was beaming at her. Not even the sun could have looked on her as brightly and warmly as he did now.

Lawrence stepped forward and unfastened the handcuffs from around Molly's wrists. "Well," he said to her. "You truly are fully of surprises."

Molly could not think what to say to him, so she said nothing. She did not speak as Mr Bennet led her out of the courtroom and toward a waiting carriage. He held out his hand to help Molly climb up, and Molly gaped at it for a moment before even realising he was offering her his assistance. She had never been in a carriage before. She had never even been in a horse-driven cart, let alone these large rectangular contraptions with roofs and windows and curtains out of which rich children might peer. Carriages were things that Molly had to remain alert for, to dodge out of the way when they came careening down the street. They were not something she rode. Yet here she was.

The inside of the carriage was even grander than the outside had suggested, with soft, plush seats more comfortable than any bed Molly had ever slept on, and red velvet curtains hanging over the windows. As Mr Bennet pulled the door closed and shouted to the driver to depart, Molly felt herself beginning to blush. She must look frightful, covered in grime. She had been in that cell for days, and she had hardly been clean and tidy before her arrest. Neatness was not her first priority on the streets, and the idea that she was dirty or messy had never bothered her before, but now, sitting on this man's fine seat, she felt incredibly self-conscious. He wore expensive clothes, and he was neat and clean. She must smell terrible. The stench of her would seep into the carriage, and he might never be rid of it. She had never felt so out of place in all her life.

But Mr Bennet did not seem to be thinking of any of that. As the carriage jerked into motion, he turned to take in Molly again, and tears of joy glistened in his eyes. For a moment, he seemed speechless.

"I—I'm Molly," Molly said after a moment.

"Molly," Mr Bennet repeated. "Yes. Emilia—your mother—she would have liked that name. It suits you."

"What—what name did she give me?" Molly asked quietly.

Mr Bennet shook her head. "That doesn't matter now. Your name is Molly. You're Molly, and you're here."

"Mr Bennet," Molly said. "I wonder... what makes you so certain that I am your daughter?"

"As soon as I saw you, I knew in my heart that it was true," Mr Bennet said. "Please, look at this picture of your mother. You will know the truth upon looking at it, I know." He held out the locket he had shown to the judge, and Molly carefully took it from him. Inside was a portrait of a young, very fine-looking woman in her early twenties. Molly felt no immediate spark of recognition in her heart, like she might have hoped, but she had to admit that the woman looked remarkably like her. In fact, the woman in the portrait could easily have been mistaken for her at first glance, and only the additional maturity in the woman's face would have told the difference on closer inspection.

Molly felt tears forming in her own eyes, and she blinked them away. Could it really be true, then? Was she looking at the face of her mother?

She passed the locket back to Mr Bennet before she could cry.

"Now, I understand this will be difficult," Mr Bennet said. "You must have had a very difficult life until now and grown up very much by yourself. It will be a matter of some adjustment, if you choose to remain with me. But I dearly hope that you will. I don't expect you to be the little girl I lost, Molly. You are your own independent woman now. It is easy enough to see that. But I should like to get to know you, and help you grow further, as much as I am able."

Molly smiled at him. He spoke to her like she was an equal, worthy of respect. Very few people had ever spoken to her that way before, and certainly not rich men such as him. She felt herself warming to him. It could not be proved whether or not he was her father, but he believed so, and he seemed like a good man. She did not think she had chosen poorly.

"How did you come to be in the courthouse?" Mr Bennet asked. "The man I spoke to said you were arrested for pick-pocketing."

Molly shrugged, feeling suddenly a little self-conscious. "I had to eat," she said. "Me and my sister—not my real sister, by blood or anything, but as close as—we worked together. I got caught so that she could escape."

"That sounds very selfless of you."

"Well, I didn't *intend* to get caught," Molly said. "I thought I could get away. But if one of us was going to be caught, I'm glad it was me and not her."

"Well, I am glad it was too. I might never have found you."

The carriage slowed to a halt, and Mr Bennet smiled. "Here we are," he said. "Home at last."

The carriage door opened from the outside, and Mr Bennet gestured for Molly to climb out ahead of him. She was a little shaky on her feet as she clambered down, and she could not stop herself from gasping in awe at the home that stood before her. It could not possibly be the house of one man. It was enormous. It stood separate from the street, behind a tall stone wall and a sweeping green lawn, with white walls and black beams. She could see four floors worth of windows, including the little ones peeking out from the tiled roof. Ivy grew up the walls, and as Molly watched, a man in the neatest suit Molly had ever seen stepped out of the front door.

"This is your house?" Molly asked Mr Bennet, breathless.

"It is your house now," Mr Bennet said, "if you would like it to be."

The man in the suit walked down the main path and opened the metal gates that separated the garden from the street. "Welcome home, Mr Bennet," he said, with a bow.

"Mr Pertins," Mr Bennet said. "A miracle has happened. Allow me to introduce you to my daughter, Molly."

If Mr Pertins was surprised by the declaration, he did not show it. Instead, he bowed at Molly as well. "A pleasure to meet you, miss," he said. "My name's Mr Pertins. I am the butler here."

"Hello," Molly said faintly. Her father had a *butler*. If she had understood correctly, she also now had a butler. It could not be real.

Mr Bennet guided her along the path and through the front door.

The inside of the house was even more overwhelming than the outside had been. The entrance hall was warm and cosy. A large grandfather clock ticked out the seconds next to a hat stand displaying several fine hats. The floor was a gleaming dark wood, and the staircase had a sweeping wooden bannister. A portrait of the woman who Molly now recognised as her mother looked over the small landing, before the stairs turned and climbed again.

"Here, now," Mr Bennet said. He led Molly down the hallway and through a door to the left. Again, Molly could not help but gape. This room was full of fine furniture, with incredibly comfortable-looking couches and armchairs all placed to face the large, intricate fireplace. A small golden-coloured clock stood on the mantelpiece, and a large painting of horses running through a wild field hung above it. A glass-doored cabinet displayed several exotic looking trinkets on its shelves, and heavy floor-to-ceiling curtains hung over the large front windows, keeping in the warmth. Molly thought she had never felt so cosy in all her life.

She also felt incredibly out-of-place. Even breathing in this room seemed to present too much of a risk, in case any of her dirt and grime transferred to the upholstery.

Mr Bennet looked at Molly with tears in his eyes. Molly did not know what to say. Surely, she could never be good enough to belong to a place such as this.

Footsteps clattered outside, and a plump, middle-aged woman wearing an apron bustled into the room. "Can it be true?" she exclaimed. "Mr Pertins just told me that your daughter has been found!" She looked around the room, and her eyes widened when she saw Molly. She beamed. "Dear me!" she said. "Here she is and looking just like her ma used to. Why, you could think Miss Emilia were back here once again."

"Miss Jenkins," Mr Bennet said. "This is Molly, my daughter."

"Molly," Miss Jenkins said, beaming. "And what a lovely child you are. My name is Miss Jenkins. I'm the maid of the household, and it is lovely to meet you."

Molly was lost for words. None of this felt like it could truly be real. She had woken up in a prison cell, facing retribution from Mrs Snorleigh, and now she was standing inside the grandest house she had ever seen, with a man claiming to be her family, and every stranger beaming to see her. It was overwhelming.

Molly opened her mouth to greet Miss Jenkins, but no sound came out.

"Oh, dear," Miss Jenkins said. "You must be exhausted. Come along with me, now. We'll run you a nice hot bath. How about that?"

A *hot* bath? Molly had never experienced such a thing in her life. But it would be nice to get the dirt off, at least. Then she might feel slightly less out of place. She nodded, and Miss Jenkins bustled forwards and put a gentle, guiding hand on her shoulder. "Come along then," she said. "I'll show you where your room is to be."

# CHAPTER 5

The hot bath was a revelation. Molly had never felt so warm and comfortable in all of her life. The heat of the water warmed her chest and relaxed the tension in her muscles, making it easier to breathe, and the feeling of Miss Jenkins gently working soap into her hair made her eyes fall closed.

"You must've had a tough life," Miss Jenkins said, as she rinsed the soap from Molly's hair. Her hands were gentle and kind; something about her touch made Molly believe that she could trust her. "Have you been living on the streets?"

Molly nodded. "It wasn't so terrible," she said. "I had people with me."

"Oh, I wish your ma had lived to see you again," Miss Jenkins said. "Seeing you really is like seeing her again."

"When did she die?" Molly asked softly.

"Ten years back now," Miss Jenkins said. "She was always a little frail after you were taken away from her, the poor dear. And once the consumption settled in her lungs, she faded far too quickly."

"I wish I could have met her," Molly said softly.

"Oh, she's with us," Miss Jenkins said. "Even if she can't speak to us. I've no doubt she's watched over you these past few years. Might well have been her influence that brought you and your father together."

"As—as a ghost?" Molly asked.

"A spirit," Miss Jenkins said. "When you get to my age, Miss Molly, and you've seen the things I've seen, you learn that those who depart this world are never truly gone. They still pop back in every now and again, to keep an eye on us, until we're ready to join them in the kingdom of Heaven."

Molly closed her eyes. Could that be true? Had her mother been with her all this time? She could feel tears burning in her eyes. It felt horrifically unfair, to be reunited with her family, and for her mother to have already passed on. She wanted to speak to her, to hold her. But perhaps she had never been alone after all. Perhaps, along with Boots and Hazel, she had had a mother's love too.

"What was my mother like?" Molly asked.

"Oh, a kinder woman you'd never meet," Miss Jenkins said. "So charitable, with a smile for everyone. A gentle soul. You always felt like she was truly listening to you as you spoke. That she truly felt for you. I think perhaps it was all the pain that *she* had suffered, miss. It made her heart particularly sensitive to the suffering of others, and she would do anything she could to help them."

"She sounds like a good woman," Molly said.

"Oh, that she was, miss," Miss Jenkins said. She squeezed the excess water from Molly's hair and wrapped a towel around the ends. "There now. All clean. I'll get some supper made up for you, Miss Molly, and then might I suggest you get a little sleep? It's been an eventful day."

Molly nodded and allowed Miss Jenkins to gently dry her and dress her in a loose, silky smooth nightgown. Miss Jenkins tucked Molly into the largest and softest bed Molly had ever seen, and despite everything that had happened, Molly found herself drifting off to sleep at once.

$$\sim$$

WHEN MOLLY AWOKE, for a moment she thought she must still be in a dream, or that perhaps she had died and moved on to Heaven. She had never felt so comfortable in her entire life. She felt as though she were floating on a bed of clouds, with the softest of silks wrapped around her.

Then she heard footsteps nearby, and the rustle of material, before sunlight poured across her. Molly blinked and took in the room around her.

Where was she? She was lying in a huge bed, with sheets and blankets piled atop her. The walls around her were deep green and decorated with white flowers, and they weren't covered with paint, she quickly realised, but a delicate paper. The door and the skirting board were both a deep, solid wood, and opposite the bed she saw a dressing table with a fine-looking jug balanced atop it.

An older woman stood by the large windows, pulling back the thick material that covered them to let the sunlight in. *Miss Jenkins*, Molly remembered slowly, like she was recalling the details of a story or a dream. She was not at Boots's, or in a cell. She was in Mr Bennet's house. He was wealthy, and he claimed to be her father.

It could not all have been true. But Miss Jenkins gave no indication that she realised she should not have been there. She bustled toward Molly and pulled back the sheets. "Good morning, Miss Molly. I hope you slept well?"

Molly sat up, not knowing what to say. But Miss Jenkins was already bustling over to a wardrobe and pulled out what seemed to Molly to be a number of dresses. "Let's get you dressed, my dear," she continued, "and down to breakfast with your father. He's eager to see you."

Molly allowed Miss Jenkins to dress and arrange her as she desired, utterly clueless as she was regarding what Mr Bennet's daughter should look like. But there seemed so very much of the clothing. In the streets, she had worn loose-fitting rags, and counted herself lucky that she had the clothes and the warmth that she had. But being dressed by Miss Jenkins was a seemingly endless task. First there was the white linen shift that gently brushed Molly's skin, and then the corset atop it, with laces up the back that Miss Jenkins tightened to support Molly's not-particularly-generous bust and pull in her stomach. Once it was tightened and tied, Molly felt transformed, although she was not certain it was for the better. Her breathing felt shallower, and the lacing kept her back and shoulders perfectly straight, preventing her from falling into her usual comfortable posture. A person couldn't run away from the police in such a contraption, or climb a fence, or even really bend down to pick something off the floor.

Miss Jenkins then dressed Molly in a white petticoat, with lace around the edges, before tying a strange cage-like metal contraption around her waist. Molly spun slightly on the spot, watching it sway around her with amazement, and Miss Jenkins laughed, before pulling a thick, deep red dress over the top.

Molly stared at her own reflection in the mirror as Miss Jenkins brushed and pinned her hair. She looked like one of the fine ladies that Molly sometimes saw on the streets, the ones she often targeted for some trick or scheme. She had not known that they wore ridiculous metal cages beneath their skirts to create that wide, pavement-filling silhouette, but unless Miss Jenkins was playing a cruel joke on her, it must be true. No wonder those women walked so slowly and so daintily, and never put up a chase when robbed of their purse. The layers felt as though they were weighing Molly down and taking a single step would be a masterful act of balance and care. The hairpins dug into Molly's scalp as well, pulling her hair up into a style that transformed her into a girl who was truly a stranger.

Was this who she was to be now? She was not certain that she liked it.

But, she supposed, it was far better than prison or the workhouse. If it pleased her father, she would learn to accept it for his sake.

Molly walked stiffly down the stairs after Miss Jenkins was finished, flinching when the cage beneath her skirt bumped against the bannister. Her father was already seated in a room that Miss Jenkins called the breakfast room—an entire room, just for breakfast! But he stood when Molly entered, a nervous smile breaking out across his face.

"My dear," he said. "I trust you slept well?"

Molly nodded, unsure what to say. Mr Bennet gestured at the chair beside him, and when Molly approached it, he pulled it out from the table to grant her room to sit. Once she was seated, he sat himself, and gestured at the food.

Surely, Molly thought, the food in front of her could not all be for her. When Miss Jenkins pulled the silver lid off the plate, she revealed rashers of bacon and eggs, along with some kind of fish, and freshly baked bread. Molly carefully picked up the utensils on either side of the plate. They felt clunky in her hands, but she was determined to use them. They were the only things stopping her from wolfing down the entire meal in seconds. It was more food than she had ever been given at one time in her entire life.

Mr Bennet watched her eat with a slight smile on his face. He seemed to sense that it was best not to interrupt her. But as soon as the last morsel of food was gone, he leaned forward, curiosity dancing in his eyes.

"Now, Molly," he said. "I hope you will trust me with a little more information about yourself. I have missed you for over eighteen years. I would dearly like to know what your life has been all this time, even if it has been unpleasant."

Molly clutched her hands in her lap and considered how to answer. Her immediate instinct was to hide how truly low her life had been from this elegant man, for surely, he would not want her once he knew the truth. But then she remembered how he had found her, locked up and on trial for theft. He already knew that she had come from the workhouse, and about part of her criminal past. He had met her while she was wearing filthy rags, a common pickpocket being dragged through the court, and he had recognised her and accepted her at once. She could trust him with the truth.

So, speaking slowly, she began to inform him of the details of her past, as she remembered it. She took care not to mention any names, in case doing so led to consequences she could not yet see, but still she told Mr Bennet about the workhouse, about the attack and being lost on the streets and finding Hazel and Boots. He asked many questions about her life in Haven, and she felt herself livening up as she described the shared meals, the camaraderie, the different tricks they used to take down a mark. Mr Bennet listened attentively, so that every moment, Molly felt more interesting, more engaging, than she ever had before. When she finally finished her tale, he considered her for a moment, and then nodded, wiping tears from his eyes.

Molly felt an immediate spike of panic. "I am sorry," she said quickly. "If I have offended you—"

"No," Mr Bennet said. "No, it is I who have offended you, Molly. You are a brave, kind-hearted, intelligent girl, just as your mother was. You have faced your situation more than admirably. But it is heartbreaking to hear how you have struggled. That life should never have been yours. If I had done my duty to protect you, if I had found you once you had been stolen, none of it would have been."

Molly considered his words for a moment before replying. "I

suppose in such a world, I would not know any different or better," she said, "and I would probably be quite content. But I am content in the life that I have led, Mr Bennet. I wish I could have known my mother, and it was often unpleasant, but I had good people around me, and a friend who was and is more of a sister to me than any true sister could be. I would not give that up now for the world."

Mr Bennet dabbed at his eyes. "You are a wise child, Molly," he said. "I only hope I can make amends for the past now." He put his handkerchief back in his pocket and smiled. "I have been invited to a dinner party tonight. I would love if you would attend with me."

"A dinner party?" Molly repeated.

Mr Bennet nodded. "I am eager to reveal my daughter to the world."

"I—if you wish it, I will go," Molly said, "but I have never been to a party of any sort in my entire life. I would not know what to do."

"It is not so difficult," Mr Bennet said. "And you are so charming and engaging. I am certain you will be a natural. So, tell me, my dear. Will you attend with me?"

And so, Molly agreed.

*M*olly had thought dressing for breakfast with her father was a time-consuming affair, but preparations for the dinner party soon rid her of that notion. The skirt cage for the evening was even larger, and Miss Jenkins fussed over her hair for what seemed like hours, using so many pins that Molly felt she had become more metal than hair.

Mr Bennet, whose clothes had seemed so fine to Molly before, also dressed up for the occasion, and the sight of him in his taller hat and dinner jacket made Molly's heart tremble at what sort of people the evening might introduce her to.

"But how am I to act?" she asked her father, as the carriage began to rattle its way through the streets. "What do they expect of me?"

"Act as yourself," Mr Bennet said. "That is all I wish."

But was that all everyone else would wish of her? Molly did not believe so. If it was enough to simply be herself, then she would not have been dressed as extravagantly as she was, so that, nimble street orphan though she was, she now struggled to walk. At best, she could be an amusement, an oddity in this world of refinement. But if her father believed in her and wished her to attend, then attend she would.

The carriage pulled up outside a grand-looking town house, and her father helped her to step down onto the pavement. He held out the crook of his arm for her, and Molly took it tentatively, mimicking the stance she had seen fine ladies take when walking about town with a gentleman for company. Her father rapped smartly on the door, and a moment later it was opened by a man in a fine-looking suit.

"Ah, Mr Bennet," the man said. "The rest of the party is in the drawing room. Allow me to accompany you."

Molly glanced at her father, hoping he would give her a clear sign of how to act. But he simply put a hand in the small of her back to guide her inside without a word.

To Molly, the drawing room seemed very grand indeed, and the people inside it even grander. Mr Bennet immediately steered Molly toward an older gentleman with white whiskers and a small, delicate woman who seemed to be his wife. "Hugo, my boy," the man said. "What a delight to see you!"

"It's a pleasure as always," Mr Bennet said. He held out his hand, and the older man shook it firmly. "Mrs Layton, I do hope you're well."

The older woman smiled. "Quite well, Mr Bennet, thank you. And who is it you've brought with you tonight?" She gave Molly a slightly suspicious look.

"Ah," Mr Bennet said. He nudged Molly forward. "This is my long-lost daughter, Molly."

"Long lost?" Mr Layton asked, with a look of surprise.

"Indeed," Mr Bennet said. "It is a somewhat fantastical tale, but all true, I assure you."

"Then I look forward to hearing it."

"Molly," Mr Bennet said, "this is Clarence and Victoria Layton, two of my very good friends."

"It's nice to meet you," Molly said. She stuck out her hand, the way her father had done, but Mrs Layton did not move to take it. She looked down at it and raised her eyebrows slightly.

"Yes," she said, somewhat distantly. "You as well, to be sure."

Her father laughed. "She is a little new to society," he said. "I'm certain her presence tonight will be most refreshing."

Molly dropped her hand, feeling her cheeks colour slightly. She understood that she must have made some rather large mistake, but she could not for the life of her think what it must be. She had copied her father exactly.

"And will you be staying with your father long, Miss Bennet?" Mr Layton asked, with a kindly smile.

It took Molly a moment to realise that *Miss Bennet* meant *her*. She had never had a family name, not once in her entire life, and it sent a thrill through her to hear it now. "As long as my father will keep me, Clarence."

Surprise flickered across the man's face, although he tried to hide it. Again, she did not know what she had done. She resolved not to speak, not to even *move*, unless it proved absolutely necessary. It would be the best way to avoid embarrassment.

But such a resolution was not to be. Her father seemed to consider it vital to introduce Molly to every person in the room, and each of them had politely phrased questions for her that left Molly's brain in knots as she tried to decipher what the correct answer must be.

When they were seated for dinner, the servants brought in several long, covered dishes and arranged them in the centre of the long table. They removed the covers with a flourish, revealing piles of delicious food beneath. Molly watched the others around the table carefully to figure out what she was expected to do. But once Mr Layton moved to serve both his wife and himself, the others also began to reach for the dishes, and so Molly did the same.

Her stomach rumbled at the smell of the food, despite the

tightness of her corset around it. She leaned forward to reach one of the farther dishes, and her corset pressed against the table edge as she stretched. She dragged the dish closer, and then began to pile food onto her plate.

Again, she felt people watching her. She looked up to see the other guests observing her out of the corners of their eyes, judging her without wishing to appear as such. She felt herself blush again. She quickly sat back in her chair, and then her eyes fell on the trail of gravy she had left across the tablecloth. Her face began to burn, and she looked self-consciously down at her plate.

Soon the conversation picked up again, however, and Molly began to eat. There were a wide range of knives and forks arranged around her plate, and it was difficult to know which to use for what, but Molly imagined that the variety must simply be to give you some choice. The rich liked superfluous things, she knew. She ate quickly, looking straight down at her plate, hoping that if she said nothing, and looked at no one, she would not make any further mistakes.

"Miss Bennet," the woman sitting across from Molly said, when the conversation lulled. "How is it we have not met you before? Have you been away at school, I wonder?"

"A bluestocking!" another man said with a chuckle. "Perish the thought."

"An education is good for a young lady," the first woman said firmly. "It broadens one's mind and gives one the faculties to take care of oneself and one's family through all the difficulties that may arise. Do you not think so, Miss Bennet?"

Everyone fell silent, and Molly realised they expected her to give them an answer. She took another mouthful of dinner, in the hope that the food might fortify her, and then responded. "I wasn't at school," she said. "I've never been, although I'm certain it's good, as you say. I was living on the streets."

The man opposite stared at the food in Molly's mouth as she talked, a look of barely concealed disgust on his face.

"The streets?" the first woman asked. "My goodness."

"It wasn't so bad," Molly said. "I got along well enough."

"My daughter is a very brave girl," Mr Bennet interceded, with a smile. "She has had a life most of us could not conceive, and now finally she has been returned to us. And how is your son, Mr Smith, doing at Eton?"

The conversation swiftly moved away from Molly, and Molly continued to look down at her plate, certain that she had done terribly wrong, but without the slightest idea how to repair it.

When Mr Bennet declared that they really must be going, Molly immediately sensed two things: they were leaving remarkably early, and the other dinner guests were relieved to see them gone. She looked at the ground as her father said his goodbyes, not daring to say a word. Her father guided her back to the carriage, and Molly could barely breathe. She had failed. She had humiliated her father, without knowing how she was doing so, and now he had seen who she really was, and how she did not belong in his world. How would he react? Would he punish her? Throw her out of the house entirely.

Molly managed to hold her silence until the carriage started moving, and then her panic burst out of her. "Please don't send me away," she said. "I know I embarrassed you. I know I did badly. I'll learn to do better, I will. Please don't tell me to leave."

"Molly, my dear," Mr Bennet said. He took her hand in his. "I would never dream of sending you away. I must apologise to you. I was so excited to share you with the world that I did not think how it might affect you. Of course, it was overwhelming for you. There have been so many changes."

Molly nodded. She could feel tears burning in her eyes, and she blinked them furiously away.

"Do not worry yourself, my dear," her father said. "You did your best. I am certain you will learn the rules once you are given the opportunity. And I believe I know just the woman to help us."

# CHAPTER 7

The woman Mr Bennet spoke of arrived the very next day. Mrs Debauche was from France, a place Molly's father told her was a separate country across the sea, where no one spoke English and there was no royalty at all. Mrs Debauche certainly spoke English in a manner that Molly had never heard before, and she had heard all kinds of accents during her life. She spoke very precisely, in a nasal tone. She was tall and thin, her grey hair pinned atop her head in a large bun. The wrinkles on her paper-thin skin suggested she was somewhat elderly, but she radiated force of will that suggested she was not a woman to be trifled with.

Molly liked her immediately. Life on the streets had given her an appreciation for strength of character and a no-nonsense attitude, and Mrs Debauche clearly had both attributes in abundance. She looked Molly up and down upon meeting her, her eyes settling on the stubborn slouch in Molly's shoulders, despite the assistance of her corset, on the placement of her feet and the way that Molly looked away from her as she was introduced. Then Mrs Debauche smiled.

"Well," she said, in that unusual accent of hers, "you will be quite the challenge, no? But I do adore a challenge." She reached out and gently pushed up Molly's chin with her slender fingers. "Do not worry, my dear. The most important attribute a lady requires is to have a bright and kind soul, and your soul, Miss Bennet, shines clear for all to see. We will work on the manners, on the whims that society dictates to us, but the foundation is solid indeed. You will do well."

Molly smiled. She attempted to give Mrs Debauche a curtsey in gratitude, but her feet got tangled in the hoops of her skirt, and she stumbled.

Mrs Debauche's smile grew. "Perhaps we will begin," she said, "with introductions."

From then onward, Mrs Debauche visited Molly once a week to teach her the rules and expectations of polite society. The instructions seemed to Molly never ending, a false concern invented by those who had no real troubles to occupy them, but she was eager to live up to her father's trust in her, and so she listened diligently and memorised all she could. When Mrs Debauche brought Molly a few etiquette books to read, Molly was forced to admit that she did not even know the letters in her own name, and soon a reading tutor was employed as well.

On the days that Mrs Debauche visited, Molly always ended up exhausted, her mind full of all the rules and corrections she had been taught. Mrs Debauche insisted that practice was the only way to transform theory into habit, and so Molly continued to attend dinner parties, along with afternoon teas with Mrs Debauche and outings to promenade at the park or to various entertainments. Each setting had its own rules, and Molly stumbled many times, but Mrs Debauche was always patient and encouraging with her, and slowly Molly began to gain confidence. The barely concealed looks of surprise grew rarer, and the shock and disgust she had read in people's faces at that first dinner party soon disappeared.

Molly often thought about her old life, about Boots and Hazel, but she tried to content herself with what she had now. The people at Haven would hardly recognise her if they saw her now, and she suspected that some might be angry at her apparent abandonment of their lifestyle and morals. When once she had been embarrassed to find herself in polite company, she now felt she would be embarrassed if she came across the Haven crowd again, so much had she changed. But Molly knew she was making her father happy, and that had quickly become the most important thing in the world to her.

"Today," Mrs Debauche said, a few weeks into Molly's education, "I believe it is time we spoke about young gentlemen."

"What about them?" Molly asked. She had grown up in Haven with boys and girls alike, and so although the concept of calling a boy her own age a gentleman was almost laughably unfamiliar, she did not consider them strange and foreign creatures requiring particular attention.

"We must discuss how to properly engage with a young man who appears to be offering his compliments to you. What is acceptable, what is not, how to encourage him properly if you appreciate his attentions, and how to discourage him politely if you do not."

Molly laughed. "I can promise you, Mrs Debauche, that will not be necessary."

"Oh?" Mrs Debauche asked, one eyebrow raised. "And why do you believe that?"

"Because it is true," Molly said. "I am a workhouse girl, a street rat. A criminal, even! I am doing my best in my lessons, Mrs Debauche, truly I am, and I hope I can make my father proud, but no young man would wish to flirt with me in earnest."

Mrs Debauche gave her a knowing smile. "You were once a workhouse girl, it is true," she said. "And some young men will wish to take advantage of that fact, which we must guard against. But you are also now a beautiful, and rich, young woman. One with a tragic past and a very different perspective from the usual pretty and eligible girls these young gentlemen meet. You will have many suitors vying for your hand soon enough. In fact, I would be surprised if they are not vying for it already, without you noticing it."

The thought seemed ridiculous to Molly, and she laughed, but when Mrs Debauche continued to look at her in earnest, she shook her head in disbelief. "It cannot be so," Molly said. "I never once imagined I would get married. I do not have suitors."

"Even so," Mrs Debauche said, still smiling, "let us prepare for such an eventuality, especially if such attention proves unwanted."

Once Mrs Debauche put the suggestion in Molly's head, however, Molly began to notice the way the young men acted around her. Many gave her curious or even subtly appreciative glances, and as time went on, more and more men approached her for conversation or even to ask her for a dance.

But if this was the thrill of romance, Molly rather thought that she could continue to live without it. Her would-be suitors, if she could truly call them that, were remarkably dull. Some talked to her about their own wealth, their horses, their estates, their ambitions, without giving Molly a chance to say a word, while others showered Molly with compliments and seemed ready to cater to every whim she might share. Molly was particularly careful in rebuffing this second group. The first sort of gentleman was tedious, yes, but their self-admiration was at least genuine, and she imagined she could learn something about this society from them. The second sort were entirely facetious. They were self-absorbed in their own way, and Molly immediately understood that they flattered her in an attempt to win her, or, more precisely, to win the money they imagined she had, due to her father.

"I still do not think I will marry," Molly said to Mrs Debauche one day, "not even if I were to receive a hundred proposals. These young men are all incredibly boring. They only like me for my money, and do not care one whit about who I am as a person. Some, I think, could not even comprehend that I *am* a person, with opinions of my own. I would rather never speak to a young man again then endure another evening like that."

But Mrs Debauche merely smiled. "Indeed," she said, "many young men are blinded by money, whether they have it or simply desire it. The rules and techniques we are learning help you to identify that, and to extricate yourself from those situations."

"It is not just *some* situations," Molly muttered. "Every one of them is a fool."

"You believe so, Miss Bennet?" Mrs Debauche asked. "We shall see, I suppose."

DESPITE MOLLY'S many outings with Mrs Debauche and her father, she began to feel restless. She was accustomed to roaming free, to spending time by herself and watching the city from the shadows, and although she was grateful to her father for all he had given her, she sometimes missed the liberty that her old life had allowed her. Mr Bennet seemed deeply worried that some accident or misfortune might befall his daughter, separating him from her once again, so he never allowed her to leave the house unattended. Even when she was at home, Molly often found herself with company, and she rather thought her father had requested that Miss Jenkins keep a close eye on her when no one else was around.

It warmed Molly's heart to feel wanted and protected, but she also began to feel a little stifled by all that had changed. She wished for time to herself, to breathe the fresh air and look at the sky and not be concerned with any of the rules or expectations for a while.

And so, she began to ask her father if she might take short walks outside the house by herself. At first, her father was reluctant, citing concerns for her safety, before invoking Mrs Debauche's opinion on 'propriety'. Mrs Debauche, however, seemed to both see and understand Molly's need, and she told Mr Bennet that a young lady such as Molly needed a little freedom, and that indeed short walks by herself would be a boon to her constitution.

With his excuse regarding propriety dismissed, and realising, perhaps, that his protests were grounded more in fear than in reality, Mr Bennet eventually relented. And so, Molly began to take the occasional solitary walk, while her father waited in his study, pretending to work, while in truth listening desperately for the sound of his daughter's return.

MOLLY WAS COMING to the end of one such stroll when she looked up, lost in her thoughts, and saw a familiar face walking toward her. It was the policeman who had arrested her and then later cared for her while she was locked away.

Mrs Debauche had not given Molly specific rules for greeting a policeman who had once chased you down after a theft, but Molly, startled by his sudden appearance, did what she could.

"Mr Carter," she said. "What a pleasure to see you again. I hope you have been keeping well?"

Lawrence stared at her for a moment, taking in the elegance of her posture and the finery of her dress. "I am well, thank you, Miss Bennet," he said, with a bow. "May I express my surprise at seeing you?"

"You may," Molly said with a grin. "I'm surprised to see you as well."

"It seems as though I knew you from another life, Miss Bennet. You are much changed since we last met."

She looked down, blushing slightly. "Society is new to me," she said, "but I hope to make my father proud."

"Then I am certain that you will," Lawrence said.

She offered him a polite smile. It felt strange to be conversing with him in the language usually reserved for dinner parties where she still did not quite fit in, but the words flowed much easier when she saw Lawrence's friendly grin.

"I must thank you, Mr Carter," she said, "for your kindness to me. You did me a great service when we met."

Lawrence scratched the back of his neck, blushing slightly. "It was no trouble, Miss Bennet," he said.

"No," Molly said, the word slipping out despite her training. "I believe it must have demanded a great deal from you. You helped me when I was most desperate, and I—thank you, sir."

"Well, then, you're welcome, Miss Bennet," he said. "I was happy to help and would do so again." He glanced around, a regretful look crossing his face. "Unfortunately, Miss Bennet, I am on patrol at the moment, so I should not linger. But it was a great pleasure to see you again."

"You as well," Molly said. Lawrence bowed and began to walk away, but she called after him. "Do you patrol this area frequently, Mr Carter?"

"Semi-frequently, Miss Bennet."

"Then I hope I shall see you again soon," she said, with a smile.

He bowed again. "I look forward to it," he said.

Molly walked slowly the rest of the way home, a smile playing across her face. When she reached the front door, she realised that Mrs Debauche was standing in the doorway,

smiling at her. Molly blushed, afraid she was about to get repri-
manded for speaking to a policeman so freely.

"You've learnt well," Mrs Debauche said, her smile growing,
and she beckoned Molly inside for the next lesson to begin.

# CHAPTER 8

That evening, Molly sat by the fireplace with her father, practicing her sewing while Mr Bennet read. In those quiet moments, just the two of them, the rules of polite society faded away, behind the need to spend time together and to connect. Molly sat on the floor next to the roaring fire, her sewing on her lap, while her father sat in his armchair a few steps away.

After a while, however, Molly realised that her father had looked up from his book and was watching her sew with a fond smile on his face. When she gave him a curious look, his smile grew. "You remind me so much of your mother," he said. "She would sit close to the fire to do her embroidery, or to read her novels, and the firelight shone off her hair exactly as it shines off yours. She was an excellent woman."

"I remember her sitting in that chair in the evening," he continued, glancing at an unoccupied armchair now placed on the other side of the room, "with you in her arms, rocking you, singing to you, telling you all about the world and all the wonderful things she believed you would do. It truly broke her when you were stolen. She loved you very much."

"I wish I could remember," Molly said ruefully. "I cannot recall anything from before I was in the workhouse. I think it would have given me great comfort, if I had known."

"I deeply regret not being able to find you and bring you home to your mother," Mr Bennet said. "I never stopped looking for you, knowing that your mother's dying wish was for you to be found and brought home again, but how can one small girl be found in a huge city such as this? Children go missing or become orphans every day."

"Of course," he continued, "there are also unscrupulous villains in this world, who will use a man's suffering against him. Some conmen tried to trick me, in the past. They lied that they knew where my daughter was and could return her to me, in order to extort money from me. They knew nothing, of course." Darkness flickered across her father's face. "They were dealt with, as was just. They may still be in prison for their lies. But justice does not lessen the pain of it."

Molly shivered, and her father blinked and forced himself to smile. "I am sorry, my dear," he said. "I did not intend to become so melancholy. Such tricks and lies cannot hurt us now." He reached forward and took Molly's hand, squeezing it gently. "I am so glad you are with me again."

He released her hand and stood. "I find myself more tired than I anticipated," he said. "I believe I will retire for the night."

Molly nodded and bid him goodnight, and he departed, leaving her to look into the dancing flames in the hearth and regret.

SEVERAL DAYS LATER, Molly took another walk alone around the neighbourhood. Although she would not have admitted it to anyone, perhaps even herself, she secretly hoped she might encounter Lawrence Carter and have the pleasure of another few minutes of conversation with him. She had no reason to plan a meeting, but she found that she wanted to see his warm, gentle smile again.

The air was cool, and Molly pulled her cloak tighter around her to ward off the chill. The sky was a cloudless grey, the air was clear, and Molly felt invigorated by the crispness of the day. The walk offered her no sign of Lawrence Carter, but as she was yet to glimpse any police officers, she held out hope that he was the one on duty in the area, and that she simply had yet to encounter him. But once almost an hour had passed, Molly began to worry that her father would miss her, and be concerned for her in her absence, and disappointedly started to think about making her way back home.

It was that moment that she heard a whisper behind her. "Girl!"

She knew that voice very well indeed, although she had not heard it in months. She spun around, eyes darting into the shadow of the alley she was passing. Boots emerged. He looked just as he always had, and Molly felt startled for a moment that he was the same, while everything about her had changed.

"Boots!" she cried. Her first instinct was to throw her arms around him, so delighted was she to see him, but she hesitated when she saw the twist of his face and the sharp look in his eyes. In all her life at Haven, Boots had only ever looked at her kindly, and truly he had been the closest thing to a father she had ever had until Mr Bennet came back into her life. But he loomed now, stepping a little closer than was comfortable, his arm coming to rest on her elbow.

"You come along with me, now," he said, and the words almost sounded like a threat. Molly's instincts told her to scream, to fight her way out of his grip and run as far and fast as she could, but surely that was ridiculous. This was *Boots*. He pulled on her arm, leading her deeper into the shadow of the alley, and she followed him, stumbling slightly.

Once they were out of the view of the street, Boots released her, and she turned to face him properly. "Boots," she said again. "Are you all right? How is Hazel?"

Boots spat noisily on the ground at her feet. "Pah!" he said. "The girl's well enough, not that you truly care."

Molly felt herself flushing. "Of course, I care," she whispered.

"Really?" Boots asked. "We haven't heard a peep from you in months. We could be dead, for all you knew. But you never thought to check after your dear sister or old Boots, now, did'ya, girl?"

He spoke the truth, and Molly felt immediately ashamed. "I am sorry," she said. "Truly I am."

"Don't speak to me with your fine words," Boots said. "What a pretty little thing they've made you, reciting their words and doing tricks for their amusement."

"I'm sorry," Molly said again. "I got so caught up in this new world that I forgot—"

"Ha!" Boots said. "Caught up in your lies, more like."

"My—my lies?" Molly repeated. There was something truly terrible in Boots's expression now, a triumphant cruelty that she had never glimpsed before, and her heart raced.

"Conning that rich man, making him believe you're his daughter. A rat like you! Somehow you've pulled it off."

"It's not a con!" Molly protested. "He said it himself. His daughter was stolen from him!"

"But that lassie ain't you, now, is she?"

Molly looked away, blushing. His words struck the fear she had kept deep inside herself, that she could not be the person Mr Bennet believed, that none of this could be true. But Boots could not know the truth any more clearly than she did. "You don't know that," she said.

"Oh, I do," Boots said. He loomed closer, leering. "I know, because I was the one who stole that man's daughter away."

Molly stared at him for a long moment, trying to make his

words make sense. It could not be true. *Boots*, the man who had saved her, the man who had protected her....

"You just got lucky," he continued, "that you look so like my Hazel. But it was never you."

The meaning clicked into place in her head. "Hazel is Mr Bennet's daughter?" she whispered.

"She was," Boots said. "She's my daughter now. And there you are, putting on airs, living in luxury in her place."

Molly felt as though she was about to be sick. "Why?" she asked faintly. "Why would you take her away?"

"I had my reasons," he said.

Molly took a step backward, toward the street. The world was spinning around her. But Boots darted forward and seized her wrist with a bruising grip, holding her in place. "Wait a moment, missy," he said. "This is valuable information, don't you think? So I think you're going to come back here with money, and you're going to pay me to keep quiet about what I know."

"*Pay* you?" Molly repeated. It still did not make sense. Hazel should have been here. It was Hazel, all along. She had to run and tell her at once. Why would she pay Boots to lie to her?

"Mr Bennet has had encounters with thieves and ruffians before," Boots said, in the tone of one making a grand, ponderous speech. "People trying to take advantage of his loss. Do you know what happened to them, girl? Your life at the workhouse will seem like luxury compared to what would happen to you if he found out you'd deceived him."

"But I didn't mean to," Molly said. "I didn't know."

"Too late now," Boots said. "I hold the power to ruin your life. So, you come back here, first Saturday of every month, and you bring me enough money to make it worth my keeping quiet. Otherwise, all it would take is one anonymous tip to the police, and it will all come crumbling down."

He released his grip on her wrist, but for a long moment,

Molly did not move. All she could do was stare at him, utterly speechless.

"Your lies will be the ruin of you, girl," he said. "But they'll be the fortune of me. Run along now. I know you won't breathe a word of this to anyone."

As if only just realising she was free, Molly turned and ran. She tore down the streets, dodging passers-by. Her hat flew off, and her hair began to fall out of its pins, but she did not slow down to fix it. Her heart was pounding wildly in her chest, and she needed to run, to get as far away from Boots and his leering face as she possibly could.

*Lies*, she thought. It was all lies.

She turned onto her own street, and then stopped suddenly, just in time to prevent herself colliding with Lawrence.

"Miss Bennet," he said. "Whatever is the matter?"

She was crying, she realised. Tears ran down her cheeks, and her whole body was shaking. She must have looked truly mad. She shook her head, stepping around him. "I am all right," she said.

"Begging your pardon, miss, but you don't look all right to me."

She shook her head again. "I have to go," she said, and she set off running again, down the street, through the gate and up the steps to the house. She did not wait for the butler to open the door for her, or for anyone to acknowledge her return. She raced up the stairs to her room, the world blurring around her, and locked the door before collapsing face first onto the bed and bursting into sobs.

It had all been a lie. An unintentional lie, but a lie none-theless. She had not found her true family. She did not have a father and a late mother who loved her. She was as alone in the world as she had ever been—more alone, now she knew the truth about Boots—and the pain of losing that hope, after dreaming of it for so long, was almost worse than never having felt it at all.

And worst of all, she had stolen her dear Hazel's happiness. She had stepped into a position of luxury that should always have been Hazel's, had basked in love that truly belonged to her. But to tell the truth would devastate Hazel, not delight her. She truly believed that Boots was her father. The discovery that the man who had raised her was the worst kind of liar and crook would break her heart.

But, Molly thought, as she cried, she was merely making excuses. She knew that justice meant telling the truth about what she knew. She could not allow Boots to blackmail her or live a lie in order to receive Mr Bennet's misplaced love. But once she spoke about what she knew, she would lose everything. If she was lucky, she would return to the street. But Mr Bennet would be furious. He would feel humiliated, after introducing her to society, despite her flaws, and insisting that she was his long-lost daughter, finally found again. Surely, he would want retribution against the street rat who had deceived him.

Molly did not know what to do. She did not know what she *could do*. So, she lay on her bed and cried, while first Miss Jenkins, and then Mrs Debauche knocked on the door and inquired after her health. Molly didn't respond to either of them. Miss Jenkins returned later and told her that she had left hot tea and toast outside the door, for if Molly was hungry, but Molly did not move to collect it. Her despair weighed her down, trapping her in the blankets, and she cried until she could cry no more.

It must have been deep into the night when Molly heard a light knock on her door. It wasn't the way Miss Jenkins or Mrs Debauche had knocked.

"Molly?" It was Mr Bennet's voice. He sounded worried, but his voice remained soft and calm. "Molly, are you all right?"

Molly couldn't bring herself to respond. How could she? She was afraid that if she opened her mouth, she would begin weeping all over again. She couldn't lie to him, so for now, her only option was silence. Silence and waiting.

Mr Bennet didn't open the door, but Molly didn't hear him leave either. A muffled sigh came from the other side of the door. "It's times like this that I really wish Emilia was still with us." The sadness in Mr Bennet's voice was overpowering. "She would always know what to do in a situation like this. She was amazing when it came to helping people. She always knew the exact right thing to do. I so wish you could have met her, Molly."

A tear rolled down Molly's cheek. She wished she could have met her mother—no, Hazel's mother as well. Especially if she'd know the right thing to do, because at the moment, Molly had never felt more lost.

"You remind me of her so much," Mr Bennet continued. "Not just in the way you look, Molly, but in the way you act. You have that same goodness in you..." Mr Bennet trailed off again. There was another pause in which Molly could feel herself yearning to speak out, begging for help, but she couldn't.

"If..." Mr Bennet searched for the right words to say, "If I have done anything wrong to offend you, I am deeply, deeply sorry, and I will do anything to rectify it."

Mr Bennet waited another minute or so for a reply. On receiving none, he wished Molly a good night, hoped she slept well, and took his leave.

Molly had never felt so alone before.

# CHAPTER 9

*T*he sun dawned the following morning, but Molly's life did not seem any brighter. Her troubles were unchanged, and after her display of tears and despair, everyone in the household knew that something was amiss. They would question her, and she would either be forced to lie, or forced to admit the truth and lose everything.

She splashed water on her face and dressed herself in as simple clothes as she could find in Miss Bennet's wardrobe. Then she heard a knock on the door.

"Miss Molly?" It was Miss Jenkins. She sounded deeply concerned, and Molly felt a rush of guilt at the concern that she had caused her. "A policeman is here to see you." Molly's stomach dropped, and she swayed on her feet. The police? Had Boots contacted them already? "His name is Mr Carter," Miss Jenkins added. "He says he is an acquaintance of yours. He much desires to speak with you."

Molly felt a rush of relief, but it was short lived. Mr Carter had seen her distress the previous day, and she was certain that she owed him an apology for the rude way she had spoken to him. And what would he think of her when he learned the truth? He would believe she was just a common criminal, not worth his affection, and he would regret all the time he had wasted in their acquaintance thus far. The thought of his smile turning to a look of disapproval and disgust made her want to weep.

"Miss Molly?" Miss Jenkins said again. "He's waiting in the breakfast room. Are you available to meet with him?"

Molly might have been a liar and a crook, but she was certainly not a coward. She would not hide away in her room and force others to worry about her, especially when she truly did not deserve their concern.

"I will be down in a moment, Miss Jenkins," Molly said. She struggled to make her voice sound calm and even.

"Do you require any assistance getting ready, Miss Molly?" Miss Jenkins asked.

Molly shook her head, even though Miss Jenkins could not see. "I am all right, Miss Jenkins," she said. "I will be down soon."

"Well, if you're certain, Miss Molly," Miss Jenkins said. She did not sound convinced.

Ten minutes later, hands shaking, Molly descended the stairs and walked into the breakfast room. Lawrence stood by the window, illuminated by the streaming sunlight as he looked out onto the street.

"Miss Bennet," he said, as soon as she emerged. "I am so relieved to see you. I apologise if my coming here is improper, but I was concerned about you after yesterday. Are you well?"

"Yes, Mr Carter," Molly said, and she was surprised by how steady her voice was. "I am quite well. I must apologise for my rudeness yesterday. I was not myself."

"Please, Miss Bennet. No apologises needed. But you seemed greatly distressed."

Molly twisted her hands in front of her. Even downplaying her feelings was lying, in a way, and after all of Lawrence's help and kindness towards her, it felt wrong to withhold any truth from him. Until now, her lies had all been unwitting. If she continued now, then it was a choice, and that felt like a far greater sin.

But how could she speak the truth, with all that it would cost her?

"Miss Bennet?" he asked.

"Molly," she said. "Please." She took a couple of steps toward him and then stopped. "What would you do," she asked, "if you knew a secret that could put you in danger if it was revealed? Would you tell the truth, so that justice could prevail, or would you remain silent and keep yourself safe?"

Lawrence stared at her. "Molly," he said. "Whatever is going on? If you are in trouble—"

"Please," Molly said. "Tell me."

Lawrence was quiet for a long moment, and she could tell he was considering the question. "I would like to think," he said slowly, "that I would do the right thing. I would tell the truth and hope that those I am closest to would be there to protect me."

"And if you had no one to protect you?" Molly asked.

"Molly," Lawrence said again. He took a step towards her, reaching for her hand, and then stopped himself. He looked at her with concern. "What has happened? Please, Molly. You can trust me."

Molly considered him for a long moment. His eyes were full of concern. Perhaps she could trust him. He was a policeman, but he had helped her before, when he knew nothing about her. Perhaps he could advise her or work to make the punishment less harsh. Assuming he believed that she had been unwitting in the scheme, of course.

"I would like to," Molly said. "But I am afraid."

He stepped closer again. "Afraid of what?"

The door to the breakfast room swung open, and Mr Bennet strode inside. Lawrence backed away from Molly at once, restoring a respectable distance between them. Mr Bennet raised an eyebrow at their closeness, but he did not comment. "Miss Jenkins informed me that a policeman was here to see my daughter," he said instead. "I trust that everything is all right?"

Lawrence glanced at Molly, as though trying to read in her expression what to say. "I hope that is the case," he said slowly. "But I was concerned, Mr Bennet. I saw your daughter yesterday afternoon, and she appeared greatly distressed. I wished to inquire after her health."

"I wish the same," Mr Bennet said. "The entire household was greatly concerned for you, Molly. Perhaps Mr Carter here can help to explain what is occurring?"

"I wish that I could, Mr Bennet," Lawrence said. "But I am lost as to the cause myself."

Molly took a deep breath. The moment had come, far quicker than she had expected it. She could not lie outright to Mr Bennet, not after all his generosity and kindness toward her. She could only hope that Lawrence would protect her from Mr Bennet's wrath.

"I want to explain, sir," she said, "but it is difficult to begin. Yesterday, I learned—I was informed—I am not truly your missing daughter, sir. Your daughter is a girl called Hazel. She lives in the city, with a beggar known as Boots."

For a long moment, nobody spoke. "What has led you to believe this?" Mr Bennet asked.

"Hazel is my friend," Molly said softly. "She is the girl I told you about, and the man pretending to be her father… he is the beggar who saved me, a man known as Boots. He cornered me on the street yesterday and told me the truth—that I cannot be your true daughter, because he was the one who took her, and he knows her to be Hazel. I am so sorry, Mr Bennet."

Her whole body trembled. She could not bear to look at him.

"But you look so like your mother," Mr Bennet said softly.

"Hazel and I have always looked like sisters," she said. "I wish I had realised it before."

She waited for Mr Bennet to explode in anger, to swear at her and banish her from this house, or to demand that Lawrence arrest her at once. Instead, he just shook his head.

"And you are certain?" he said.

Molly nodded. "He did not seem to be lying to me, sir," she said. "And we have always looked remarkably alike."

Mr Bennet turned to Lawrence. "Mr Carter," he said, and Molly flinched. "If this story is true, then my daughter may be in danger. Please, will you help me to find her and bring her home?"

Lawrence glanced at Molly. "I will, sir," he said. "If this Boots has revealed the truth to Molly, he must have some manner of plan afoot."

"Indeed," Mr Bennet said.

Molly quickly described the last location of Haven. "We did not move around much," she said. "They are likely still there."

"Then that's where we will go," Lawrence said. He gave Molly another concerned look. "Please wait here, Molly. We don't know what danger we may be walking into."

"Yes," Mr Bennet said distractedly. "Molly must remain here. Come, Mr Carter. There is no time to waste."

And without another word, the two gentlemen rushed from the house.

# CHAPTER 10

*L*awrence Carter was having a most unusual twenty-four hours. He had not caught a glimpse of Miss Molly Bennet for several days, and even though he knew that the daughter of the great Mr Bennet would have no interest in a lowly policeman like him, he was eager to see her. She had seemed pleased to see him when chance had brought them together, so he had hope that a friendly acquaintance might be possible between them, even if that was all it could ever be.

But when he had seen Molly racing down the street, her face wet with tears, his heart had broken for her. He had been desperate to find out what had happened, but she had run past him with hardly an excuse, and he had told himself that it was not his place to interfere in her affairs any longer.

But the sight of her panicked face would not leave his thoughts. What if, he thought, she truly was in trouble? What if somebody had hurt her? He was a policeman, after all. He was equipped to help her in a way that few could. By the time morning had come, he had been resolved. He had hurried to her home and hoped that she would forgive him for his impertinence.

He had never imagined the truth. A man had told Molly that she was not Mr Bennet's lost daughter at all, and that he had been the one to steal the true baby away. They needed to act quickly. Molly seemed terrified that admitting the truth would lead to terrible consequences. Plainly, the thief had threatened her into silence. Perhaps he had even threatened harm on the real stolen girl. She had seemed to be a friend of Molly's, from childhood. Molly had intervened to save a girl on the day he had met her. Could that have been who they were discussing?

There was no time to lose. Leaving Molly in the safety of her home, he and Mr Bennet raced across London to the address that she had provided. Molly's information led them to an abandoned-looking building.

"We should be cautious," Lawrence said to Mr Bennet, as they approached. "The criminal could be waiting for us inside."

Mr Bennet ignored him. He was so desperate to see the girl that he ran straight inside without a moment's hesitation, forcing Lawrence to run after him.

The inside of Haven was filthy, but Mr Bennet did not seem to notice. He raced through the inside, glancing at the few inhabitants without pausing, and then suddenly came to a stop and gaped at the girl who had stood up to greet him.

Lawrence vaguely recognised her as the girl who had been with Molly on the day of her arrest. The two of them did look remarkably alike, he thought. Their hair and facial structures were similar, but it ran deeper than that. The two girls had spent many years growing up together, and it had led to a similarity in stance and mannerisms that was truly uncanny.

"What can I do for you, sirs?" Hazel asked. Her words were perfectly polite, but her tone was full of subtle defiance.

Mr Bennet did not reply. "It is true," he said. "It is you."

"How can you be certain, sir?" Lawrence asked. "You believed Molly was your daughter too."

"Molly resembles my late wife, it is true," Mr Bennet said.

"But now I know the truth. In my heart, I know. Even her presence in the room is similar to my late wife's."

"Molly, sir?" Hazel asked. She darted forward, looking desperate. "What do you know about Molly? I haven't heard from her in months. Is she all right? Is she in trouble?"

"She is well," Lawrence said quickly. "Do not worry."

Hazel looked at him, and then she narrowed her eyes. "You're the copper who chased her," she said. "What did you do to her?"

"I did my job, miss," Lawrence said. "And it set off the strangest series of events."

"Hazel," Mr Bennet said softly, his voice awed. "Please, listen to me. My name is Mr Bennet. I know this will come as a shock to you, but I believe I am your father."

"That cannot be true, sir," Hazel said, in a soft and slightly scared voice, as though she thought Mr Bennet might be slightly mad. "I have a father."

"I believe you have been lied to," Mr Bennet said. He hurriedly explained all that had happened, and Hazel's eyes grew wider and wider as she learned about her friend's fate. It was clear that, although Boots had known Molly's whereabouts for some time, his daughter had not heard a word.

"But it's impossible, sir," Hazel breathed. "My pa must be lying, to trick Molly into giving him money. He was so angry when she left us. She was his best worker, you see."

"That may be true," Lawrence said. "But would you consider returning with us, so that we can investigate? Molly is waiting for you."

Hazel glanced between Lawrence and Mr Bennet. "My pa will be furious," she said.

"Where is your pa?" Lawrence asked gently. "The man they call Boots?"

"He left, sir," Hazel said. "He said he heard that a policeman was on his way here, so he went to stop them."

"That is strange," Mr Bennet said. "We saw no one matching his description on our journey here. Certainly, no one attempted to delay us."

"Molly!" Hazel said, with a gasp. "He was so furious with her. If he thinks that she has spoken out and ruined his plan... I do not know what he might do, sir. I would never have thought him capable of hurting dear Molly, but if all that you say is true... he is not kind to those he thinks have betrayed him."

Lawrence stared at Hazel in horror. If the events of the previous day were any indication, then Boots knew where Molly lived. And now she was in the house alone, with no one to protect her. If Boots truly thought she had thwarted him, if he thought she had cost him money that he relied on... she was not safe.

Without a word, Lawrence turned and ran for the house.

# CHAPTER 11

*M*olly paced her bedroom, despairing over what to do. Soon, she knew, Mr Bennet would return with his true daughter. This room would become Hazel's room. These dresses were truly Hazel's dresses. Everything that Molly had enjoyed over the past several months truly all belonged to her friend.

Molly did not resent her for it. Hazel was deserving of all the most wonderful things in life, and she knew Hazel would be as delighted with Mr Bennet as Mr Bennet would be with her. But Molly knew that she was now simply waiting for the fairy tale of the last few months to end. If she was lucky, Mr Bennet would simply cast her back out onto the street, and then where would she go? She could not return to Haven and Boots. But she feared punishment for deceiving Mr Bennet, even unwittingly, for being part of another con against him. Would she be locked away? She supposed it was what she deserved. Mr Bennet had been the one to save her from jail in the first place, and that had only been because he had believed she was someone she was not.

The best thing, perhaps, would be to leave now, before Mr

Bennet and Lawrence returned. It would save her the pain of the inevitable rejection and keep her safe from the arrest that otherwise seemed inevitable. She reached for a bag to begin packing, and then stopped, tears burning her eyes. None of the possessions in this room truly belonged to her. If she took them when she departed, she would not only be stealing from Mr Bennet, who had been so kind to her, but from Hazel as well. Yet her old dress from the streets had long since been turned to rags, and she could not run out naked. She would need to take one dress. The simplest one.

She began to walk toward the wardrobe, and then jumped when she heard a crash of breaking glass from downstairs. What on earth could that be? She hurried onto the landing, overtaken by worry about Miss Jenkins, and then froze when she heard the maid's scream.

"Where's the girl?" a gruff, familiar voice shouted. "Upstairs?"

It was Boots.

Boots had broken into the house, Boots had attacked Miss Jenkins, Boots was searching for her.

Molly's first instinct was to run down the stairs and give Miss Jenkins her aid. But the maid had already fallen silent, and Molly could hear Boots making his way through the house. The best thing that Molly could do to assist Miss Jenkins was the best thing she could do to protect herself—run. Flee as far away from this place as possible, knowing that Boots would follow her, praying that she could manage to evade him.

She ran down the stairs, reaching for the front door, but halfway across the hall, Boots lunged into view. He looked much worse than he had even a day before. His beard looked patchy, his eyes were bloodshot, and he stank of liquor and desperation.

"There you are," he said.

He moved quickly, crowding Molly from the side, so that she

could neither reach the front door nor run down the entrance hall without moving into his reach. Her only option was to run back up the stairs again. She turned and ran, and she heard the pound of his feet as he ran after her.

Several knickknacks decorated the stairway, rich frivolities that Molly had marvelled at when she had first arrived. She seized them now as she ran, first a vase, then a small metal bust, next a lamp, and threw them behind her as she ran with all her might. Boots made a grunt of pain, suggesting she had hit her mark, but she did not pause to look.

Her efforts did not even make him hesitate. She might have slowed him down slightly, given herself a fraction of a second of time, but his footsteps thundered after her, as determined as before.

Molly dove into her room and slammed the door behind her. She turned the key in the lock and then scrambled away, frantically looking around the room for anything she might be able to use to defend herself.

Boots slammed against the door, and the whole room shook. "Girl!" he shouted. "You can't hide from me!"

He kicked the door, hard, and the lock broke. The door flew open, and Boots stumbled into the room. His face was flushed, his eyes too big, as he looked at her.

Molly threw a book at him, as hard as she could. He dodged it nimbly, but otherwise did not react.

"You've ruined me, girl!" he shouted. "You want to take my daughter away from me? All I wanted was a little money. All I wanted was a little SECURITY. I worked hard all my life to protect you, and this is how you repay me?" He lunged for her, and Molly dodged, scrambling as far out of reach as she could.

"It isn't right," Boots spat. "I want *justice*."

"Justice for you would be a lifetime in jail!" Molly cried. "You stole Hazel from her real family. Why?"

"I've lost too much," Boots spat. "My own girl, dead. My wife dead with her. And these rich businessmen, who already have so much in life, so much they don't deserve—why should they have what I can't? Hazel is *mine*. And so are you."

He lunged for her again. Molly tried to dodge him again, to dart for the door, but she was far less nimble in her fine dress than she had been even at her worst in her street rags, and she could not move fast enough. Boots' hand wrapped around her wrist, squeezing hard enough to bruise, and Molly gave a cry of pain and fear.

"Let me go!" she shouted, but Boots was beyond reason. His other hand seized her by the throat and began to tighten.

"You betrayed me," he spat. "You stole from me. Did you think you could get away with that? Did you?"

Molly struggled against him as hard as she could, fighting desperately for air. She needed to get free, Boots seemed certain to kill her, but the tighter he squeezed, the harder it was for her to summon the strength to resist. Her limbs grew heavy. The world around her grew dim. She didn't have the air to scream or spit, and her legs flailed uselessly as Boots dragged her by the neck as easily as if she were a rag doll.

Then a shadowy figure appeared in the doorway. Molly could not see who it was, and when she tried to let out a cry of desperation, she barely made a sound.

The figure lunged at Boots with a cry of fury, wrenching him away from Molly. The last thing that Molly saw, before she lost consciousness, was Lawrence's face.

# CHAPTER 12

*W*hen Molly awoke, she was lying in a large, soft bed. Her throat hurt terribly, and her whole body felt heavy, so for a moment she resisted waking up altogether, tempted by the comfortable oblivion of sleep.

Then, images came to her mind. Boots chasing her. His hands on her throat. The darkness that had swallowed her up. And the figure, her rescuer, bursting into the room to save her.

Molly opened her eyes and sat up. She was in her bedroom, beneath the familiar pile of blankets. Mr Bennet had not yet thrown her out. She had been granted at least a slight reprieve.

She touched her neck gingerly. The skin felt swollen and sore.

Then she noticed the young gentleman in the armchair beside her. Lawrence sat just out of arm's reach of the bed, fast asleep. He had dark circles under his eyes, and even in rest, he looked tense and worried.

"He wouldn't leave you, Miss Molly," a voice said. Molly looked at the doorway, where Miss Jenkins stood. The maid had a bruise on the side of her face, but she otherwise looked well. "He said he didn't care a whit about propriety, that he couldn't possibly leave your side until he knew you were all right. Even the doctor couldn't reassure him."

"Miss Jenkins!" Molly said. "Are you all right? I heard you scream!"

"Yes, my dear," she said. "I am well. A bit startled, and I regret that I was not more help, but I'm a tough old thing."

"I'm so sorry, Miss Jenkins," Molly said. She moved as though to rise from the bed, but her body still felt heavy, and it resisted her efforts. "This is all my fault."

"Nonsense, child," Miss Jenkins said. "Not a part of it was you. It was all that man, and his willingness to hurt anyone in his way. You cannot be held responsible for that. He was the one who wished to hurt you. You are the victim in this, my dear, not the guilty party."

Molly wanted to argue with Miss Jenkins, but before she could speak, Lawrence stirred.

"I'll fetch you a nice hot drink, miss," Miss Jenkins said. "And give you and the young man a chance to talk."

She bustled away, leaving the door open behind her.

As soon as Lawrence saw that Molly was awake, he sprang to his feet and hurried to her side. "Molly!" he said. "Thank goodness you're awake. I feared the worst."

"I am well," she reassured him. "Just tired."

"I cannot apologise enough," he said. "If I had not left you unattended—if I had returned faster—I allowed you to come into harm's way. I cannot forgive myself."

"You saved my life," Molly said. "It was you I saw, wasn't it, before I fainted?"

"Yes," Lawrence said, "that was me, and almost too late—"

"You were not too late," Molly said. She reached out and took his hand. "You saved me."

Lawrence smiled. "You no longer need to worry," he said. "Boots has been arrested. He cannot hurt you anymore."

But although Molly was glad to be safe from Boots,

Lawrence's statement simply reminded her of the trouble that she was still very much in. She pulled her hand from his and clutched the top of the bed sheet nervously.

"What will happen to me now?" she said softly. "I no longer have a family. I have nowhere to go."

The smile fell of Lawrence's face. "I do not know," he said. "But I am certain Mr Bennet will want to see you, as soon as he learns you are awake."

"Then please, don't leave," Molly said. "I do not know how to face him alone."

"I will stay," Lawrence said. "But Molly, I don't think—"

Whatever he did not think, he never got the chance to say. Before he could finish the thought, a loud voice cried from the hallway, "Molly!"

Hazel barrelled into the room, her expression desperate. She launched across the room, tears in her eyes, and threw her arms around Molly. "I am so sorry, Molly," she said. "I should have realised. I should never have trusted him. I would never have imagined he might try to kill you. Please, forgive me."

Molly held her friend, who she had not seen in months, never wishing to let go. For Hazel to beg for *her* forgiveness, after all that had happened… "I am the one who should be begging for forgiveness," Molly said, and her voice shook as tears began to roll down her cheeks. "I have behaved terribly. I took what was yours. If I had insisted on contacting you after arriving here, if Mr Bennet had seen you, none of this would have happened."

"You met Mr Bennet because you sacrificed everything to save me," Hazel said, squeezing Molly even tighter. "You have done nothing wrong. But I have missed you terribly. Please, never go far from me again."

Molly heard more footsteps in the hall and looked up to find Mr Bennet entering the room, smiling. "I see you are awake," he said to Molly.

Molly felt herself pale. How could she meet Hazel's desperate request, when she was surely about to be banished from the house? Hazel must have thought the same thing, because she released Molly and turned instead to face her father.

"Father," she said. "Please don't be angry with Molly. She did not know the truth, any more than you or I did. Please don't throw her out."

"Throw her out?" Mr Bennet said. He opened his mouth in surprise, and then he chuckled. "Whatever would give you that idea?"

"Don't—don't you want me to be punished?" Molly said. "For deceiving you?"

"Deceiving me?" he cried. "You did no such thing! Indeed, you put your own life at risk in order to tell me the truth and reunite me with Molly. Your bravery and honesty are both truly commendable. And did you truly think, child, that I only cared for you because of an assumed blood relation, and that otherwise I would throw you out onto the street?" Molly could not reply, but he must have seen the answer in her face, because he hurried forward, his eyes full of sympathy. "My dear child," he said. "It was the assumption of blood that brought us together, but how could I spend so many months in your company without developing true affection for you, regardless of our relationship. You are a bright spot in my life, child. I am greatly happy to have Hazel returned to me, but that does not diminish my affection for you. Indeed, I came here with the intention of officially adopting you, if you would agree."

"Adopt me?" Molly asked breathlessly. She blinked at him, her eyes still full of tears. She would not be homeless? She would still have a father and a family? A father and family who had *chosen* her, no less?

"Oh, Molly," Hazel said. She hugged her again. "Please say yes. Then we will be sisters in truth!"

The words were too much for Molly. She burst into tears, sobbing against her sister's shoulder.

"There, now," Hazel said, "don't cry. It's not *that* terrible."

Molly giggled through her tears, and Hazel laughed true. "Say you will," Hazel said again, and Molly nodded.

"Of course, I will," she said. "I would like nothing more in the world."

She released her sister and dabbed her eyes. Then she spotted Lawrence, standing uncertainly in the corner of the room. When he saw her watching him, he bowed, a little stiffly.

"I will take my leave," he said. "I do not wish to intrude."

"Nonsense!" Mr Bennet said. "You could never intrude." He strode over to Lawrence and shook his hand firmly. "You saved my daughter's life," he said. "I cannot thank you enough."

Lawrence blushed slightly. "I was just doing my job, sir," he said. "I only wish I could have helped more."

Mr Bennet—Molly's father—chuckled. "Yes," he said. "A young policeman, just doing his job to protect my girl." He glanced between Molly and Lawrence, and then he winked. "Well," he said, "I imagine you will see the need to offer her your protection rather frequently in future. In your capacity as one of the Queen's young officers, of course. I imagine, with Molly remaining here, that I will be seeing a lot more of you in the future."

Lawrence blushed even deeper, his ears turning bright red, and Molly felt herself blushing too. Then Mr Bennet laughed, while Hazel threw her arms around her sister once again, and Molly thought that finally, truly, she had found home.

# EPILOGUE

 wo Years Later

LAWRENCE CARTER RAN through the streets of London, weaving his way through the crowds. It might, he thought later, have been quicker to pause and hire a cab—he had the money for such luxuries now—but the thought of slowing down, even for a moment, was

unbearable. He felt the desperate need to act, and that meant running, as fast as he possibly could, until he reached his wife.

How could he be missing the birth of his first child? The doctor had said that Molly would not have the child for another two weeks, and yet here he was, on a sunny Thursday after-noon, receiving a missive from his father-in-law informing him that the baby was being born and that he should return home at once. If Lawrence had anticipated it, he never would have left the station and gone on patrol. He never would have left Molly's side at all.

It was difficult to believe that he was about to become a

father. He had expected it for months, of course, been delighted and terrified by the thought, utterly unable to wait until the moment he would meet his firstborn for the very first time. But that had all been rather intellectual, and knowing that his child was coming was not precisely the same as feeling it. Well, he felt it now. His heart was racing, his thoughts were rushing through his head, and he just knew that he needed to get home as soon as he possibly could, or he would surely miss it.

It felt like just yesterday that he had proposed to Molly, after months of courting her with her adopted father's permission. They had been walking in the flower gardens not far from the Bennets' house, and Molly had looked at the blooming roses with such delight on her face that all of Lawrence's plans had disappeared, and he had been unable to wait a moment longer to ask her to become his wife. She had said yes, of course, threw herself at him and hugged him so enthusiastically that the pair of them spun on the spot, both laughing with joy. Mr Bennet had granted his permission at once and had even provided Molly with an unexpected dowry that allowed the newlyweds to rent a small house in the same neighbourhood as Mr Bennet and Hazel. The wedding had been small and simple, mostly restricted to the household, as those Molly loved most, along with Lawrence's family, of course.

Almost a year later, Molly had told him that they were expecting a child. Lawrence could still remember the precise way she told him, how her voice had trembled with joy, how tears had sparkled in her eyes above her big, beaming smile.

And now the moment had come, and the two would become three.

Lawrence raced in through the front door, not even pausing to take off his coat and hat as he hurried in search of his wife.

Miss Jenkins appeared at the top of the stairs. She looked exhausted, but very happy. "Mr Carter," she said. "Come along and see."

Molly was lying in bed. She was soaked in sweat, her hair plastered to her head and her neck, but her eyes sparkled, and Lawrence thought that she was even more beautiful than she had looked on the day he first saw her. In her arms, wrapped in blankets, was the baby.

"We have a daughter," Molly whispered to him, and Lawrence's heart leapt. A *girl*. He was a father to a daughter.

She looked so small and delicate, Lawrence thought. Her skin looked impossibly soft and wrinkled. Her eyes were closed, with one tiny hand resting by her nose, but as though she sensed the presence of her father, she suddenly opened her bright blue eyes and looked directly at him.

Lawrence's heart swelled. He knew, instantly, that this was a love unlike any he had ever felt before.

"Would you like to hold her?" Molly asked. Lawrence nodded, and Molly moved the girl into his arms. She was so *small*, Lawrence thought, as he cradled the back of her head in his hand. Tears formed in his eyes.

"Hello," he said softly. The baby girl yawned, and her eyes fell closed again.

"What should we name her?" he asked Molly.

"I thought, perhaps, Emilia," Molly said. "After Hazel's mother. She is, in a way, the one who brought us all together."

"Emilia Carter," Lawrence said. "Yes. That sounds perfect."

He looked down at his sleeping daughter and smiled.

## THANK YOU FOR CHOOSING A CORNERSTONE TALES BOOK!

We hope you enjoyed the story, and as a way to thank you for choosing Cornerstone Tales we'd like to send you this free book, and other fun reader rewards…

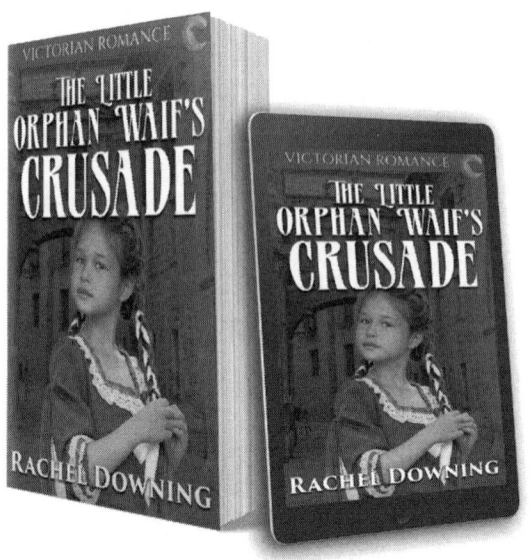

Click here for your FREE COPY of
'The Little Orphan Waif's Crusade'
**PureRead.com/victorian**

Thanks again for reading.
See you soon!

# THE FIRST CHAPTER OF 'THE WORKHOUSE ORPHAN RIVALS'

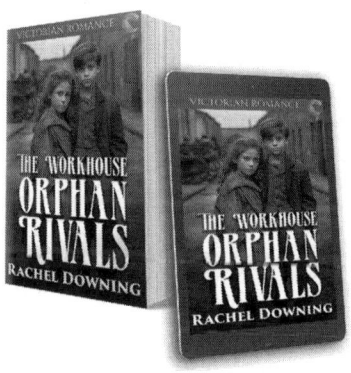

*C*harlotte Ripley giggled as she scampered down the cobblestone streets, her pigtails bouncing with each step. The warm summer sun cast a golden glow over the bustling city, and the air was thick with the aromas of fresh bread and chimney smoke.

"Wait for me!" called a voice from behind her.

Charlotte spun around, her hazel eyes sparkling, as Lucas Alcott rounded the corner. His cheeks were flushed and he doubled over, panting.

"You're too fast, Charlie," he said, using the nickname that only he was allowed to call her.

Charlotte grinned, not the least bit apologetic. "You'll have to keep up then, won't you?"

Lucas straightened, a playful gleam in his eyes. "Oh, I'll keep up all right." With that, he took off after her, his feet pounding against the uneven stones.

A squeal of delight escaped Charlotte as she fled, weaving through the throngs of people going about their daily business. Vendors hawked their wares, horses whickered, and the general cacophony of the city surrounded them, but in that moment, it was just the two of them, lost in their childish game of chase.

Finally, Charlotte ducked into a narrow alleyway, pressing her back against the cool brick as Lucas skidded to a halt in front of her.

"I caught you," Lucas panted, leaning against the opposite wall.

"For now," Charlotte countered, her eyes twinkling. "But you'll never catch me for good."

Lucas smiled. "You'll never get rid of me, Charlie."

"Over here!" Lucas hissed, gesturing towards a small nook between two buildings. Charlotte followed him, her heart pounding with excitement at the prospect of a new discovery.

Tucked away in the shadows was an old wooden crate, its contents spilling out onto the ground. Lucas knelt down, sifting through the debris with eager hands.

"Look at this!" he exclaimed, holding up a tarnished pocket watch. Its face was cracked, but the intricate engravings along the side still caught the light.

Charlotte gasped, taking the watch gingerly in her hands. "It's beautiful," she breathed, running her fingers over the delicate etchings.

Lucas grinned. "It's yours, then. It's definitely some great treasure. I'm sure it's got all sorts of mysterious hidden away in it. We'll just have to work them out."

Warmth blossomed in Charlotte as she clutched the watch to her heart. This was why she loved Lucas so dearly – he always knew how to make her feel special, like she was the most important person in his world.

Their adventures continued, each day a new escapade. One afternoon found them perched high in the branches of a gnarled oak tree, swapping stories and dreams as the leaves whispered secrets around them.

"When I'm grown," Lucas declared, "I'm going to sail the seas and see the whole world."

Charlotte wrinkled her nose. "The whole world? What about me?"

"Of course you'll come too," he said matter-of-factly. "We'll have grand adventures together, you and I. We'll never be apart."

Charlotte smiled, comforted by the promise in his words.

Then there were the days spent racing through the streets, their shouts of laughter carrying on the warm breeze. Tag was their favourite game, a whirlwind of darting bodies and breathless taunts.

These were the moments Charlotte cherished, the memories she knew she would hold dear for the rest of her life. In those carefree days of childhood, with Lucas by her side, she felt invincible, as though nothing could ever tarnish the innocence of their bond.

CHARLOTTE WATCHED her parents with admiration as they prepared for their day's work. Even at her young age, she understood the sacrifices they made to provide a stable home for her.

Robert Ripley rose before the sun, his movements quiet yet purposeful as he dressed for the docks. Charlotte heard the creak of the wooden floors as he laced up his heavy boots. When he emerged from the bedroom, his face was etched with determination, a man ready to tackle another gruelling day of labor.

"Off to earn our bread, little one," he said, ruffling Charlotte's hair affectionately. Despite the early hour, his eyes crinkled with a warm smile.

Charlotte nodded solemnly. "Be safe, Papa."

With a final nod, Robert strode out the door. Charlotte knew the docks were an unforgiving place, the work arduous and unrelenting, but her father embraced it without complaint. He was a man of quiet strength, unwavering in his commitment to provide for his family.

As the front door closed behind Robert, Jane emerged from the kitchen, her hands already busy tying the strings of her apron. "Good morning, my darling," she said, pressing a kiss to Charlotte's forehead. "Did you sleep well?"

Charlotte nodded, though truthfully, she had been awake for some time, lying in bed and listening to the familiar sounds of her parents' morning routine. It was a comforting ritual, one that anchored her in a sense of security and love.

Jane headed back into the kitchen, bustled around packing her midwife's bag with the necessary tools and supplies. Her movements were efficient yet gentle, a testament to the care she brought to her work. Charlotte knew that her mother's calling was more than just a job – it was a sacred duty, one she embraced with all her heart.

"A new babe is coming into the world today," Jane said, her eyes shining with anticipation. "Isn't that a wondrous thing?"

Charlotte nodded again, her heart swelling with pride. Her mother was a beacon of strength and compassion, a guiding light for those in need.

As Jane gathered the last of her things, she paused to smooth Charlotte's unruly curls. "Mind the house for me, won't you, love? I'll be back before you know it."

With a final kiss and a whispered "I love you," Jane swept out the door, her steps purposeful and her head held high.

Charlotte watched her parents go, their paths diverging into the bustling streets of London, and felt a profound sense of gratitude. Though their work was humble, their dedication knew no bounds. It was through their unwavering efforts that Charlotte's world remained secure, a haven of love and stability in an ever-changing city.

CHARLOTTE'S FEET carried her down the familiar path, her steps light and carefree as she made her way to Lucas's home. The warm summer breeze tousled her hair, and she couldn't help but skip a little, filled with the boundless energy of youth.

As she rounded the corner, the modest dwelling came into view—a humble abode, but one that radiated a sense of comfort and familiarity. Charlotte could already picture Lucas waiting for her, his face alight with that infectious grin that never failed to make her heart swell.

She rapped her knuckles against the weathered door, the sound echoing within the stillness of the narrow street. A gruff voice called out, bidding her entry, and Charlotte slipped inside.

The interior was simple but well-kept, a reflection of the hardworking man who presided over the household. Charles Alcott sat hunched at the small dining table, his broad shoulders straining against the fabric of his shirt as he pored over a tattered ledger. Even in repose, his frame exuded a rugged strength, forged by years of toiling at the docks.

"Mornin', Miss Ripley," he greeted, his voice a deep rumble.

He glanced up, and Charlotte was struck by the intensity of his gaze, those piercing blue eyes that mirrored Lucas's own.

"Good morning, Mr Alcott," she replied, dipping into a polite curtsy.

Charles waved a calloused hand, dismissing the formality. "None of that, now. You're like family 'round these parts." A ghost of a smile tugged at his mouth, softening the harsh lines of his weathered visage.

Charlotte lips curved upwards in response, her heart warmed by the gruff affection he so freely offered. Despite his rough exterior, there was an undeniable tenderness in the way Charles regarded her, a silent acknowledgment of the bond she shared with his son.

As if summoned by her thoughts, Lucas emerged from the back room, his face lighting up at the sight of her. "Charlie!"

Charles's expression shifted, his features melting into an unguarded display of love and pride as he watched his son approach. In that moment, Charlotte glimpsed the depths of his affection, a love so profound that it seemed to eclipse the lingering sorrow that clung to him like a shroud.

For she knew, beneath the gruff exterior and calloused hands, Charles Alcott carried a wound that had never truly healed – the loss of his beloved wife during the very act of bringing their son into the world. It was a pain that had shaped him, hardening his resolve to be both mother and father to the boy who was now his entire world.

And as Lucas threw his arms around his father in a fierce embrace, Charlotte saw it all – the love, the grief, the unwavering devotion that bound this small family together. It was a poignant reminder that even in the humblest of circumstances, the human spirit would shine through, a beacon of resilience and hope in the face of adversity.

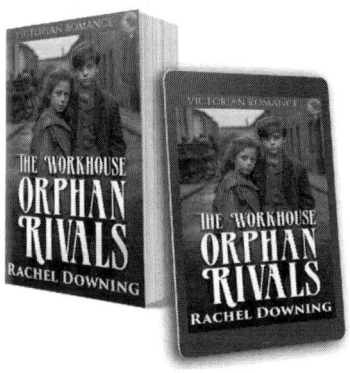

### Click here to read the rest of
### The Workhouse Orphan Rivals'

**Childhood sweethearts torn apart. A promise broken. A love that refuses to die.**

In the gritty underbelly of Victorian London, Charlotte Ripley's dreams are shattered when her childhood love, Lucas Alcott, chooses ambition over their bond. Thrust into the very workhouses she once feared, Charlotte fights to survive—never expecting to see Lucas again.

But fate has other plans.

When Lucas reappears as her new foreman, old feelings reignite amidst a powder keg of resentment and desire. Can Charlotte forgive the boy who broke her heart? Or will the dashing footman Brandon Johnson sweep her off her feet in her new life as a maid?

As secrets unravel and danger lurks in the shadows, Charlotte must decide who to trust—and who truly deserves her heart.

**From workhouse grime to aristocratic shine, this gripping**

tale of love, betrayal, and redemption will keep you turning pages long into the night. Watch as childhood promises collide with adult realities, testing the limits of forgiveness and the power of true love.

'The Workhouse Orphan Rivals'

# OUR GIFT TO YOU

## AS A WAY TO SAY THANK YOU WE WOULD LOVE TO SEND YOU THIS BEAUTIFUL STORY FREE OF CHARGE.

Click here for your FREE COPY of

'Samuel's Newfound Strength'

**CornerstoneTales.com/sign-up**

Set before '*The Button Maker's Orphan Daughter*', this story tells the tale of how Samuel met his future wife Lily, and what set him on the path to owning his very own button-shop.

At Cornerstone Tales we publish books you can trust. Great tales without sex or swearing, but with all of the mystery and romance you expect from a great story.

Be the first to know when we release new books, take part in our fun competitions, and get surprise free books in your inbox by signing up to our free VIP Reader list.

As a thank you you'll receive a copy of 'Samuel's Newfound Strength' straight away, alongside other gifts.

Click here to sign up for our mailing list, and receive your FREE stories.

**CornerstoneTales.com/sign-up**

# LOVE VICTORIAN ROMANCE?

## Other Rachel Downing Books

### Two Steadfast Orphan's Dreams

*Follow the stories of Isabella and Ada as they overcome all odds and find love.*

Get 'Two Steadfast Orphan's Dreams' Here!

### The Orphan Prodigy's Stolen Tale

*When ten-year-old Isabella Farmerson's world shatters with the tragic loss of her parents, she's thrust into a life of hardship and uncertainty.*

Get 'The Orphan Prodigy's Stolen Tale' Here!

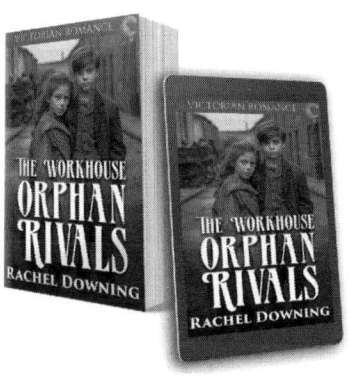

### The Workhouse Orphan Rivals

*Childhood sweethearts torn apart. A promise broken. A love that refuses to die.*

Get 'The Workhouse Orphan Rivals' Here!

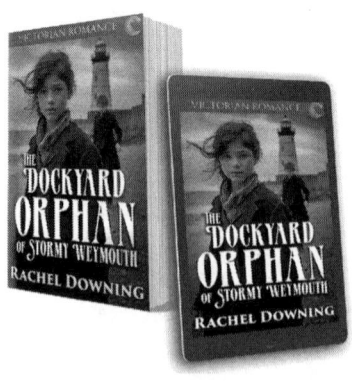

## The Dockyard Orphan of Stormy Weymouth

*Sarah Campbell's world crumbles when a tragic accident claims her parents' lives. She finds solace in the lighthouse's beam that guides ships to safety. But it's a young fisherman wrestling with his own loss, who truly captures her heart.*

Get 'The Dockyard Orphan of Stormy Weymouth' Here!

**And from our other Victorian Romance Author Dorothy Wellings...**

### The Moral Maid's Unjust Trial

*Matilda must fend for herself when her father is wrongfully accused for a crime he didn't commit.*

Get 'The Moral Maid's Unjust Trial' Here!

If you enjoyed this story, sign up to our mailing list to be the first to hear about our new releases and any sales and deals we have.

We also want to offer you a Victorian Romance novella - 'The Little Orphan Waif's Crusade' - absolutely free!

Click here to sign up for our mailing list, and receive your FREE stories.

**CornerstoneTales.com/sign-up**

Printed in Dunstable, United Kingdom

74049743R00118